SEVEN OUT
OF TIME

MORE WILDSIDE CLASSICS

Please see www.wildsidepress.com for a complete list!

SEVEN OUT OF TIME

ARTHUR LEO ZAGAT

WILDSIDE PRESS

SEVEN OUT OF TIME

Originally published in *Argosy* magazine in 1939.

This edition published in 2009 by Wildside Press, LLC.
www.wildsidebooks.com

CHAPTER 1

TIME IS OF THE ESSENCE

"YOU HAVE NOT found Evelyn Rand."

"No sir," I agreed. "But I —"

"No excuses, Mr. March." The office was enormous, the desk massive, but sitting behind the latter Pierpont Alton Sturdevant dominated both. Not because of any physical quality. He was below average in stature nor did his graying hair have the patches of white at the temples that fiction writers and the illustrators of advertisements seem to think are the invariable mark of 'men of distinction.' It was rather his hawk's nose and the sexless austerity of his thin mouth that made me think of him as resembling some Roman Emperor, and myself, a very junior attorney on the staff of the august firm of Sturdevant, Hamlin, Mosby and Garfield, as some young centurion returned from Ulterior Gaul. "You should know by this time," the dry voice rustled, "that I am not interested in excuses, but only in facts."

I had, in truth, just returned to the city, from the remote reaches of suburban Westchester, and what I had to report was failure. "The fact is, sir, that I have not found Evelyn Rand."

Sturdevant was very still, looking at me in the huge leather armchair to which he'd motioned me with a terse, 'Good morning.' He was expressionless and still for a long moment and then he asked, "If you continue searching for her, how soon do you think you will be able to locate her?"

I didn't like that if. I didn't like it at all but I contrived to keep my dismay out of my face and my voice. "I can't say, Mr. Sturdevant. I haven't been able to unearth a single clue as to what happened to her." The girl had walked out of her Park Avenue apartment house that Sunday morning, two weeks ago yesterday, and vanished. "The doorman seems to have been the last person ever to see her. He offered to call a taxi for her and she said that she would walk to church. He watched her go down the block and around the corner."

"I could not take my eyes off the lass," the grizzled attendant had told me, "though my phone was buzzing like mad. She swung along freelike an' springy like as if it was the ould sod was under her feet ate not this gray cancrete that chokes the good dirt. I was minded o' the way my own Kathleen used to come up Balmorey Lane to meet me after work was

done, longer ago than I care to think."

By the way he spoke and the look in his faded eyes, I knew I needed only to tell him what it would mean to Evelyn Rand if the fact that she had never returned — never been seen again, got out, to keep him silent. And so it had been with the elevator boy who had brought her down from her penthouse home and with the servants she had there; the granite-faced butler, the buxom cook, Renee Bernos, the black-haired and viva-cious maid. Each of them would go to prison for life sooner than say a single word that might harm her. Nor was this because she was generous with her wages and her tips. One cannot buy love.

"That is all you have been able to discover," Sturdevant pressed me.

"That is all."

"In other words you are precisely where you were two weeks ago," he murmured, "except for this." He turned a paper on his desk so that I could see it, then tapped it with a long, bony finger. "Except, Mr. March, for this."

It was a statement of account headed ESTATE OF DARIUS RAND, Dr., to STURDEVANT, HAMLIN, MOSBY & GARFIELD, Cr. Beneath this heading was a list of charges, thus:

1-27-47 — ½ hr. P. A. Sturdevant, Esq. @ $400 . . . . $ 200.00

1-27-47 — 2/10/47 88-¼ hrs. to Mr. John March @ $25 . . . . $2206.25

1-27-47 — Disbursements/expenses to Mr. John March, (acct. ¼attached) $64.37

Total $2470.62

"Two thousand, four hundred and seventy dollars and sixty-two cents," Sturdevant's finger tapped the total, "up to last Saturday. To which must be added the charge for this quarter hour of my time and yours, plus whatever you have spent over the weekend. Two and a half thousand dollars, Mr. March, and no result."

He paused but I said nothing. I was waiting for what he would say next.

He said it. "As trustee of the Estate of Darius Rand I cannot approve any further expenditure. You will return to your regular duties, Mr. March, and I shall notify the police that Miss Rand has disappeared."

And that was when I lost my grip on myself — "No!" I fairly yelled as I came up to my feet. "You can't do that to her." He wasn't the Head of the Firm to me in that moment. He was a shrivelled old curmudgeon whose scrawny neck I lusted to wring. "You can't make her a pauper. You don't know what you're doing."

I stopped. Not by reason of anything Sturdevant said or did, for he said or did nothing. I don't know how he made me aware I was making a fool of myself, but he did.

And now he said, quietly, "I know exactly what I am doing. I know better than you do that because of the embarrassment his actress wife had caused him, before she died, by trailing her escapades through the newspapers, Darius Rand's will tied up his fortune in a trust fund the income of which goes to his daughter Evelyn only as long as her name never appears for any reason whatsoever in the news columns of the public press. When she vanished I determined as her legal guardian to conceal the situation for a reasonable length of time since a report to the police must inevitably bring her name into the newspapers. That reasonable time has in my opinion now expired without any hope of her return and I no longer can justify my silence. Therefore, as trustee of —"

"The Estate of Darius Rand," I broke in. "You're measuring the happiness of a girl against dollars and cents."

The faint shadow that clouded Sturdevant's ascetic countenance might mean I'd gotten under his skin but his answer did not admit it. "No, Mr. March. I am measuring a sentimental attachment to a young lady over whose welfare I have watched for more than six years against the dictates of duty and conscience."'

"Aren't there times, sir, when one may compromise a bit with duty and even conscience?" Not him, I thought. Not this dried mummy, but I had to try to persuade him. "Give me a week more. Just the week. I'll take a leave of absence without pay, I'll even resign, so you won't have to charge the Estate for my time. I'll pay the expenses out of my own pocket. If you'll only keep this thing away from the police and the papers for a week I'll find Evelyn. I'm sure I will."

Gray eyebrows arched minutely. "It seems to me that you are oddly concerned," Sturdevant mused, "with a young lady whom you have never seen, whom you never even heard of up to fourteen days ago. Or am I mistaken in that?"

"No," I admitted. "Fourteen days ago I was not aware that Evelyn Rand existed. But today," I leaned forward, palms pressing hard on the desktop, "today I think I know her better even than I know myself. I know her emotional makeup, how she would react in any conceivable situation. I have literally steeped myself in her personality. I have spent hours in her home, her library, her boudoir. I have talked on one pretext or another with everyone who was close to her; her servants, her dressmaker, her hairdresser. I know that her hair is the color of boney and exactly how she wears it. I know that she favors light blues in her dress and pastel tones of pink and green. I have even smelled the perfume she had especially compounded for her."

In his little shop on East Sixty-third Street, the walrus-mustached old German in the long chemist's smock had looked long and uncertainly at me. "Ich weiss nicht — " *he muttered.*

"You say a friend from Fraulein Rand you are und a bottle from her individual perfoom you want to buy her for a present. Aber I don't know. Ven I say so schoen ein maedchen many loffers must haff, she laughs und says she hass none. She says dot ven someone she finds who can say to her so true tings about her as dot I say in der perfoom I make for her, den she vill haff found her loffer but such a one she hass not yet met."

"Look," I argued. "Would I know the number of the formula if she had not told it to me?"

It was from Renee Bernos I had gotten it, but the German was convinced. When I opened the tiny bottle he'd sold me for enough to have fed a slum family a month, my dreary hotel room was filled with the fragrance of spring; of arbutus and crocuses and hyacinths and the evasive scent of leaf-buds; and with another fainter redolence I could not name but that was the very essence of dreams.

For a moment it had seemed almost is if Evelyn Rand herself was there in my room . . .

"Ah," Sturdevant murmured. "What did you hope to accomplish by so strange a procedure?"

"I figured that if I could understand her, if I could get inside her mind somehow, I should know exactly what was in it when she walked down Park Avenue to Seventy-third Street and turned the corner and never reached the church for which apparently she had set out."

"Is that all you've done in two weeks?"

"This weekend I went out to the house in which Evelyn's childhood was spent. It is closed, of course, but I got the keys from your secretary. I spent most of Saturday in that house and all of yesterday."

The other rooms had told me nothing about Evelyn Rand, and now I was in the last one, the nursery. It was dim and dusty and musty-smelling, for it had been closed and never again entered after a little girl of six had been sent to boarding school because her mother had no time to be bothered with her.

I pulled out a bureau drawer too far. It fell to the floor and split and that was how I found the thing that had slipped into the crack between the drawer's side and its warped bottom, at least fourteen years ago.

As my fingers closed on the bit of carved stone that lay in a clutter of doll's clothes, battered toys and mummified insects, something seemed to flow from it and into me; a vague excitement.

And a vaguer fear.

It was slightly smaller than a dime, approximately an eighth of an inch thick and roughly circular in outline and there was, strangely enough, no dust upon it. It was black, a peculiar, glowing black that though utterly unrelieved appeared to shimmer with a colorless iridescence so that almost it seemed I held in my palm a bit of black light strangely solid. Too, it was incongruously heavy for its size, and when on impulse I tested it, I found it hard enough to scratch glass.

The latter circumstance made more remarkable the accomplishment of the artist who had fashioned the gem. For it was not a solid mass with a design etched seallike upon it, but a filigree of ebony coils that rose to its surface and descended within its small compass and writhed again into view till the eye grew weary of following the Findings.

Close-packed and intricate as were the thread-thin loops, they formed a single continuous line. True, two or three of the coils were interrupted at one point in the periphery by a wedge-shaped gap about an eighth of an inch deep, but the rough edges of the break made it obvious that this was the result of some later accident and not a Part of the original intent.

I could not bring myself to believe that any human could have had the skill and the infinite patience to have carved this out of a single piece of whatever the stone was. It must have been made in parts and cemented together. I bent closer to see if I could find some seam, some evidence of jointure.

I saw none. But I saw the snake's head.

Almost microscopically small yet exquisitely fashioned, it lay midway between the gem's slightly convex surfaces, at its very center. I made out the lidless eyes, the nostrils, the muscles at the corners of the distended mouth.

To avoid any interruption of the design, as I then thought, the reptile had been carved as swallowing its own tail.

A strange, weird toy for a little girl, I thought, and put it away in my vest pocket meaning to fathom out later what it could tell me about Evelyn Rand.

"You seem to have been making a good thing of your assignment," Pierpont Alton Sturdevant remarked, "wangling a week-end in the country out of it, at the Estate's expense."

I felt my face flush and anger pound my temples but if I said what I wanted to, what faint chance there was of persuading him to delay reporting Evelyn's disappearance would be lost. I swallowed, said, "I also talked to the woman who was Evelyn Rand's nurse and with whom she spent the summer before you sent her to college."

"And what did you learn from Faith Corbett?" For the first time a note of interest crept into his voice although his face still was an expressionless Roman mask. "What did you learn from Evelyn's old nurse?"

What I had learned he would not understand. "Nothing," I answered him. "Nothing that I can put into words."

Faith Corbett, so shrunken and fragile it seemed she was one with the shadows of her tiny cottage, had asked me in for a cup of tea. "Evelyn was a dear child," her tenuous voice mused as the scrubbed kitchen grew misty with winter's early dusk, "but sometimes I was frightened of her. I would hear her prattling in the nursery and when I opened the door she would be quite alone, but she would look up at me with those great, gray eyes of hers and gravely say that so-and-so had been there just now, and it would be a name I had never heard."

"Oh," I said. "She was just an imaginative child. And she was always alone except for you and so dreamed up playmates for herself."

"Perhaps so," the old woman agreed, "but she was no child that summer she stayed here with me, and what happened the day before she went away I did not understand and I will never forget."

She took a nibble of toast and a sip of tea and though I waited silently for her to go on, she did not. Her thoughts had wandered from what she'd been saying, as old people's thoughts have a way of doing. "What was it?" I called them back. "What happened the day before Evelyn went away to college?"

"I was packing her trunk," the old lady mused. "I could not find her tennis shoes so I went downstairs to ask her what she had done with them. Evelyn was not in the house, but when I went out to the porch I saw her on the garden path. She was going toward the gate through the twilight, and there was an eagerness in the way she moved that was new to her.

"I stood and watched, my heart fluttering in my breast, for I knew there was no youngster about that ever had had so much as a second glance from my sweet. She came to the gate and stopped there, taking hold of the pickets with her hands. Like a quiet white flame she was as she looked down the road.

"They had not put the macadam on it yet and the dust lay glimmering in the dimness. All of a sudden Evelyn got stiff-like and I looked to see who was coming.

"The road was as empty and still as it had been before, and there was no one upon it.

"The air was smoky, kind of, like it gets in the fall and there wasn't a leaf stirring, but there must have been a breath of wind on the road 'cause I saw a little whirl of dust come drifting along it. When it came to the gate where Evelyn was, it almost stopped. But it whispered away, and all at once it was gone.

"All the eagerness was out of Evelyn. I heard her sob and I ran down the path calling her name. She turned. There were tears on her cheeks. 'Not yet', she sobbed. 'Oh Faith! It isn't time yet.'"

"'It isn't time for what?' I asked her, but she would say nothing more and I knew it was no use to ask again. And the next day she went away . . ."

Faith Corbett's voice went on and on about how she rented this cottage with the pension the Estate granted her and how it was hard to live alone, but I heard her with only half an ear. I was thinking of how in that smoky fall twilight it had seemed to Faith Corbett as if Evelyn Rand were going down through the garden to meet her lover, and I was recalling how the grizzled old doorman had said, 'I was minded a' the way my Kathleen used to walk up Balmorey Lane to meet me.' And trailing across my brain had been the frightening thought that perhaps when Evelyn Rand had turned the corner into Seventy-third Street a whirl of dust might have come whispering across the asphalt . . .

"You learned nothing at all from Evelyn's old nurse?" Sturdevant insisted. "I cannot quite believe that."

"Well," I conceded, "she did make me certain the girl was unhappy and lonely in that motherless home of hers. But, as an imaginative child will, she found ways of consoling herself."

"Such as?"

"Such as writing verse." I indicated the yellowed papers I had laid on Sturdevant's desk when I came in.

The only light left in the cottage kitchen had been the wavering radiance of the coal fire in the range. So much talking had tired Faith Corbett and she nodded in her chair, all but asleep.

"Thank you for the tea," I said rising. "I'll be going along now."

The old woman came awake with a start. "Wait," she exclaimed. "Wait! I have something to show you. Something nobody but me has ever seen before." She rose too and went out of the room, the sound of her feet on the clean boards like the patter of a child's feet except that it was slower. 'I stood waiting and wondering, and in a little while she was back with a number of yellowed papers in her hand, pencilled writing pale and smudged upon them.

"Here," she said, giving them to me. "Maybe they will help you find her."

The papers rustled in my hand. I had been very careful to conceal from Faith Corbett the object of my visit and I was wondering how she could possibly know Evelyn Rand had vanished.

"Verse?" Sturdevant peered at the sheets as he might have looked at something slightly distasteful. "Poems?"

Eager as I was to pierce the dry husk of rectitude in which he was encased, I had sense enough to retreat from my intention of reading to him, in that great room with its drape-smothered windows and its walls lined by drab law books, the lines a child had penned in a sun-bright garden. He would hear the limping rhythm and the faulty rhymes; he never would understand the wistful imagery of the words, the nostalgia for some vaguely apprehended Otherland where all was different and being different must be happier.

"Poems," I assented. "They have told me more than anything else exactly what Evelyn Rand is like."

"And so it has cost the Estate almost two and a half thousand dollars to find out that Evelyn Rand once wrote poems. You haven't even located a photograph of her, so that I can give the authorities more to go by than a word of mouth description."

As far as anyone knew Evelyn never had been photographed. But, "I've done better than that," I said, triumphantly. "I've found out that a portrait of her is in existence, painted by — " I named a very famous artist but shall not, for reasons that shortly appear, repeat that name here.

"Indeed. Why did you not bring that portrait here instead of these?" He flicked a contemptuous finger at the sheaf of old papers.

"Why did you not bring it here, Mr. March?"

"Because it is in a gallery on Madison Avenue. I intend to go there as soon as you finish with me and —"

Sturdevant's frosty look checked me. "You seem to forget, Mr. March, that I have cancelled your assignment to this matter."

There it was. I hadn't changed his decision in the least. My disappointment was too keen for speech for an instant, and in that instant the Call-O-Vox on his desk grated, with its metallic distortion of human tones: "Nine-thirty, Mr. Sturdevant. Mr. Holland of United States Steel is here for his appointment."

Sturdevant clicked the switch that permitted his secretary to hear him. "Send Mr. Holland in, Miss Carter. And please make a note. John March has been granted a leave of absence without pay for one week from date. This office will do nothing in the matter of Evelyn Rand until Monday the twenty-first."

He turned to me and I swear that there was a twinkle in his eyes. "Do not forget, Mr. March," he said, using a well-worn lawyer's phrase, "that time is of the essence of this contract."

I was to recall that warning, but in a sense far different from that which he intended.

CHAPTER 2

THE PORTRAIT OF EVELYN RAND

ART LOVERS ARE NOT as a rule early risers, and so after I had purchased a catalogue from the drowsy Cerberus in the foyer and passed through the red plush portieres before which he sat, I had the high-ceiled exhibition room to myself.

Shaded, tubular lights washing the surfaces of the paintings on the walls accentuated the dimness that filled the reaches of the gallery. A decorous hush brooded here; the thick, soft carpeting muffling the sound of my feet, close-drawn window drapes smothering traffic noise from without. I passed a circular seat in the center of the floor and saw Evelyn Rand looking at me from the further wall.

Although I had never seen her pictured anywhere, as sure was I that this was the portrait I had come to see that I did not took at the gray catalogue I'd picked up a the door but went right to it.

I was aware only of her face at first, ethereal and some how luminous against the dark amorphous background the artist had chosen to give her. It seemed to me that there was a message for me in the gray, frank eyes that met mine, message somewhere beneath their surface. It almost seemed to me that the satin-soft red lips were on the point of speaking.

Those lips were touched with a wistful smile, and there was something sad about them. Somehow the portraitist had contrived to make very real the glow of youth in the damask cheeks, the lustre of girlhood in the honeyed texture of the hair, but there was, too, something ageless about that face, and a yearning that woke a responsive ache within me.

Yes, this girl could have written the poems that were locked now in a drawer of my own desk. Yes, she would be loved by everyone who had the good fortune to know her.

She must have been about sixteen at the time of the portrait. The body one sensed within the gossamer frock, a misty blue such as tinctures the sky when it is lightly brushed with cloud, was just burgeoning into womanhood. The hollows at the base of the neck were not quite yet filled.

A fine gold chain circled that neck and pendant from it was a black gem, replica of the one I'd found in the nursery. There had, then, been two of them. Odd! I looked closer. I was not mistaken. The edge of the painted amulet was marred by a wedge-shaped break. But the same accident could not have marred two artifacts in precisely the same way. Nor could the one in the portrait be the same as that I had found in the nursery. The Evelyn Rand painted here was at least sixteen as I've said and when she'd sat for the portrait the black stone I'd found had been lost and locked behind a door that had not been opened for almost ten years.

I was wrong, of course, in thinking the breaks were exactly matched. I must be wrong, yet it was with curious reluctance that I fished the gem I'd found out of my vest pocket.

It was the same. It was precisely the same as the one in the portrait.

The stroke of a tower clock came dully into the dim gallery. *Bonn-n-ng*. As if to escape from the thoughts that probed at my mind I counted the strokes. *Bonn-n-ng*. Two. *Bo-nn-n-ng*. Three. Automatically I glanced at my wrist watch. Ten o'clock. *Bonn-n-ng* . . .

"An interesting bit," a low voice murmured. "Well worth the study you are giving it."

The little man had come up so quietly beside me that he seemed almost to have materialized out of the air of the empty gallery, yet somehow I was not startled. "Yes," I responded, slipping the stone back into my pocket. "Yes, it is quite interesting."

The fellow was short, so short that the top of his head, completely bald, barely came to my shoulder. That head seemed out of proportion, seemed almost grotesquely too large for his small figure and his round face seemed to float almost disembodied in the light from Evelyn Rand's portrait, the rest of him in shadow.

His skin was yellowish and of an odd lustreless texture I should have thought of as 'parchmentlike' except that parchment is wrinkled and this skin was so smooth that I had a disquieting impression it might be artificial. There was nothing artificial about the tiny eyes that peered unblinkingly at the picture, black eyes keener and more piercing than any I'd till then seen.

"You have noticed," the little man was saying, "how painstakingly the artist has depicted every physical detail. You feel that merely by reaching out you can touch the warmth of the girl's flesh, or straighten that fold in her frock the wind has disarranged, or take that black pendant in your hand and examine it more closely."

Did his glance flash to my face at this mention of the gem, as if to trap any change in my expression before I could mask it? I could not be sure. He was looking at the portrait again and his low, clear voice flowed on.

"But I wonder if you appreciate how much of his subject's personality the artist has contrived to convey. She is not quite in tune with the world where she finds herself. All her life she has been lonely, because she does not quite belong. She has a sort of half-knowledge of matters hidden from others of her race and time, not altogether realized but sufficiently so that very dimly she is aware of the peril the full unveiling of that knowledge would bring upon her."

"What peril?" I demanded, twisting to him. "What do you know about her?"

He smiled blandly at me, answered, "I know what the artist put on that canvas for me to read. And for you. Look at it again."

I did. I saw the girl. I saw the dark, amorphous background and that was all.

"Look." I felt fingers brush lightly across my eyes but I did not resent the liberty, forgot it, forgot the little man who had taken it.

Behind the painted girl there was no longer formless shadow. There was, instead, a desolate landscape so informed with strangeness that I knew if it existed anywhere it was nowhere on Earth. And from that scene there reached out to me a sense of awe and a sense of overpowering dread.

No living thing was visible to explain that apprehension. It stemmed from the vista itself, from the grayish purple hue of its shadows, from the sky that was too low and of a color no sky should be. Most of all, however, it was aroused in me by the monstrous monument that loomed from the too-near horizon.

Black this tremendous shape was, the same strangely living black as the little stone in my vest pocket, and incredibly formed; and there spread from it an adumbration of menace of which Evelyn was as yet unaware.

"Where is it?" I squeezed through my locked larynx. "Tell me where that place is."

"Not yet." The little man peered at me with the detached interest of an entomologist observing an insect specimen. "Not yet," he repeated and it seemed to me that he was answering not my demand but the thought in my throbbing brain, the thought that Evelyn was in some nameless danger and I must go to her to save her from it. "When it is time you will come to me and learn what you want to know." He thrust a white oblong into my hand. Automatically, I glanced down at the card.

There was not enough light to read it. I lifted it to catch the reflection from the portrait — and realized that the man was no longer beside me.

He was nowhere in the room. He must have gone swiftly out, the carpeting making his footfalls soundless. *Bon-n-ng.* The tower clock was striking again. Muffled as it was, I was grateful for the familiar sound. *Bon-n-ng . . . Bon-n-ng.* It was not the half-hour that was striking, but the hour! *Bon-n-ng.* We had not seemed to have been talking nearly that long. *Bon-n-ng.* The dull sound welled into the hush of that painting-walled room. *Bon-n-ng* . . . The gong died to silence.

Six! There had been only six strokes of the clock! I had not heard the first five. That was only natural. My attention had been on the little man. The clock had struck five times before he was gone and I became aware of it.

It takes only a small distraction of one's attention to blot out awareness of a striking clock. I'd been counting those strokes an hour ago. I had counted four when the little man spoke to me, and yet I didn't recall hearing the rest of the ten at all.

Four and six are ten!

Nonsense! This I was thinking was arrant, impossible nonsense. Nevertheless my lifted hand trembled slightly as I turned it to look at the watch strapped to its wrist.

Its hands stood at ten. At ten o'clock precisely, just as they had when the little man first spoke to me.

For a long minute the shadows of that art gallery hid the Lord alone knows what shapes of dread. The painted faces leered at me from the walls —

All but one. The face of Evelyn Rand, its wistful smile unchanged, its gray eyes cool, and frank and friendly, brought me back to reason. Her face, and the fact that behind her I could see no strange, unearthly landscape but a formless swirl of dark pigment, warm in tone and texture and altogether without meaning except to set off her slim and graceful shape.

I was still uneasy, but not because of any supernatural occurrence. A fellow who's never known a sick day in his life can be forgiven for being upset when he finds out there are limits to his endurance.

For two weeks I had been plugging away at my hunt for Evelyn Rand, and I hadn't been getting much sleep, worrying about her. I hadn't had any at all last night, returning from Westchester in a smoke-filled day, coach on the nerve-racking Putnam Division. I was just plain fagged out, and I'd had a waking dream between two strokes of the tower clock.

Dreams I knew from the psychology course I once took to earn an easy three credits, can take virtually no time to go through one's mind. From what I'd learned in that same course, that I should have imagined Evelyn in some strange land, with some obscure menace overhanging her, was a symbolization of the mystery of her whereabouts and of my fears for her. The little man represented my own personality, voicing my inchoate dreads and tantalizing me wit I a promise of a solution to the riddle deferred to some indefinite future. 'Not yet', he had said . . .

It was all simple and explicable enough, but it was disturbing that I should have undergone the experience. Maybe I ought to see a doctor. I had a card somewhere —

A card in my hand was the one I dreamed the little man had given me. *It was real!* Objects in dreams do not remain real when one wakes . . .

Hold everything! There was a rational explanation for this too. The card hadn't come out of the dream. It had been in the dream because I already had it in my hand. It must have been in the catalogue. Leafing the pamphlet as I was absorbed in contemplation of Evelyn's portrait, I had abstractedly taken it out unaware that I was doing so.

I looked at it, expecting it to be the ad of some other gallery connected with this one, or of some art school or teacher. It might be the latter but it didn't say so.

All there was on the card was a name and address:

ACHRONOS ASTARIS
419 Furman Street, Brooklyn

Brooklyn.

There is something solid and utterly matter-of-fact about that Borough of Homes and Churches, something stodgy and unimaginative and comfortable about its very name. I stuffed the card among a number of others in my wallet (lawyers accumulate such things as a blue serge suit accumulates flecks of air-floated thread) and forgot it.

I took a last, long look at the portrait of Evelyn Rand. My reconstruction of her personality was complete. All that was left was to find her.

All that was left! I laughed shortly and a little bitterly as I turned to leave the exhibition room. I had hoped somehow, somewhere among the things she had touched, the people she had known, the scenes through which she had moved, to come upon a hint of where and how to look for her. I had found nothing. Worse, every new fact about her that had come to light denied any rational explanation of her disappearance.

There was no youth in whom she was enough interested to make the idea of an elopement even remotely possible. She had manifested every evidence of contentment with her way of life; quiet, luxurious, interfered with not at all by the trustees of the Estate. To conceive the sensitive, shy girl as stagestruck would be the height of absurdity.

No reason for voluntary disappearance that I had been able to think of would fit into Evelyn's makeup as I knew it now.

Foul play was as thoroughly eliminated. Kidnappers would have made their demand for ransom by this time. Seventy-third Street had been crowded with churchgoers that Sunday morning; no hit-and-run accident, with the driver carrying off his victim, could have occurred unobserved. The police and hospital records had offered no suggestion of any more ordinary casualty that might have involved her. The charitable organizations to whom the income of the Estate of Darius Rand would go were to be chosen by the trustees only after the event of a lapse of her right to it. Evelyn Rand was the last person on earth to have an enemy, secret or otherwise.

The more I had learned about her - the less explicable her absence had become. I was licked. I ought to go back to the office and tell old Sturdevant to call in the police — I stopped stockstill in the brittle winter sunshine of Madison Avenue. Tentatively, almost fearfully, I tested the air with flaring nostrils.

I had not been mistaken. Faint but unmistakable I smelled what I'd thought I had; the mingled scent of arbutus and crocuses and hyacinths and the nameless fragrance of dreams. The perfume that was used by Evelyn Rand, and Evelyn Rand alone.

She was near. She was very near. She had passed this way minutes before. Seconds, for the delicate aroma could not have lived longer in the gasoline fumes and the reek of this city street.

I looked for her. Eagerly I looked for the girl of the portrait, and saw a messenger boy slouching down the pavement, a rotund beldame swathed in mink entering her sleek limousine, business men bustling past, someone's chic secretary on her way to the bank on the corner with a deposit book held tightly in her gloved small hand. A shabbily dressed old man pored over a tome at the sidewalk stall of a used bookstore beside me. I was in the middle of the block and nowhere on it was anyone who possibly could be Evelyn Rand.

The scent was gone and I felt empty inside. Weak. People were turning to stare at me. A man in a gray Homburg hat and a double breasted dark overcoat started toward me; if he spoke to me I'd probably pop him on that clipped little triangle of beard that waggled from his chin. I wheeled to the bookstall, plucked a ragged volume out of it — anything to hide my face, to give me a chance to pull myself together.

If this sort of thing kept up I was destined for an asylum. First I'd seen, talked to, someone who didn't exist. Now I was taking to smelling things. I tried to recall if I'd ever heard of anyone having olfactory hallucinations . . .

The bookworm next to me was watching me curiously. That was because I hadn't opened the book I'd picked up, wasn't even looking at it. If I didn't do so right away he'd be sure something was wrong.

The cloth binding was blistered and water-soaked, but the lettering on it still was distinct. The title of the book was — THE VANISHED!

It was, of course, pure coincidence. Nevertheless the short hairs at the nape of my neck bristled. It was too damned pat a coincidence for comfort.

The cover almost came away from the rest of the volume as I opened it. The paper was mildewed, powdery. I found the title page. The words, *'The Vanished'*, were repeated. Beneath the Old English type was a short paragraph in italics:

"Here are tales of a scant few of those who from the earliest dawn of history have vanished quietly from among the living yet are not numbered among the dead. Like so many whispering whorls of dust they went out of space and out of time, to what Otherwhere no one still among us knows, and *none will ever know."*

'Like so many whispering whorls of dust.' Could it be pure coincidence that those words wavered on this stained page? My fingers were cold and numb as I turned it and stared at the headings; Elijah, Prophet in Israel. The Tsar Alexander the First. King Arthur of Camelot. John Orth, Archduke of Tuscany. Francois Villon, Thief, Lover and Poet. The Lost Dauphin. They Who Sailed on the *Marie Celeste*. Judge Crater of New York.

And, How Many Unrecorded Others?

Was Evelyn Rand one of the 'unrecorded others' who have vanished 'out of space and out of time?' Perhaps, the thought came to me, perhaps somewhere in this book I may find that hint, that suggestion of what has happened to her for which I've hunted so long in vain.

Not rational, of course. But remember I was not rational at that moment. Distinctly not rational, so far from it in fact that once the idea occurred to me it seemed to me that Evelyn approved, that she was urging me to act upon it.

I went into the store, shadowed, musty with the peculiar aroma of old paper and rotted leather and dried glue found only in such establishments. A gray man in a long gray smock shuffled out of the gray dusk between high shelfstacks.

"How much is this?" I inquired, holding the volume up.

"Hey?" He peered at me with bleared, half-blind eyes. "Hey?"

"I want to buy this book," I repeated. "How much do you ask for it?"

"This?" He took it in his clawlike hands, brought it so close to his face I thought he would bruise his nose. *"The Vanished?* Hm-m — " He pondered a matter of life and death. Finally he came out with the price. "Thirty-five cents."

"Little enough." I shoved my hand in my pocket, discovered I had no small change. "But you'll have to break a five for me," I said, taking my wallet from my breastpocket. "That's the smallest I have."

"You're a lucky man," the bookseller squeaked. "To have five dollars these days. Heh, heh, heh." I suppose the shrill twitter was meant for a laugh, but it irritated me. I jerked the bill from the fold so hard that it brought out with it a card that fluttered to the floor.

The gray man took the greenback and shuffled off into some misty recesses beyond the shelving. I bent to retrieve the white oblong.

I didn't pick it up. I remained stooped, my fingers just touching it, my nostrils flaring once more to the scent of spring, to the perfume of Evelyn Rand.

The sense of her presence was overpowering but now I knew it did not mean she was anywhere near. The perfume came from the card I was picking up and the printed name on that card was *Achronos Astaris.*

At last I knew where to look for her.

CHAPTER 3

SAFARI TO BROOKLYN

"HERE'S YOUR CHANGE, mister."

I thrust the card into my coat's side pocket as I straightened. "Keep it," I told the bookseller grinning.

"And keep the book too. I don't need it any more." The way he stared at me, pop-eyed, was excruciatingly funny. I laughed aloud as I strode out of that musty old store of his. I didn't know where Furman Street was — like most Manhattanites I thought of Brooklyn as some strange bourne the other side of the moon — but I'd soon find out. I looked around for a policeman, saw one standing on the corner observing a bevy of giggling young females board a bus. "Furman Street," he repeated, scratching his head. "Never heard of it."

"It's in Brooklyn," I suggested.

"Oh, Brooklyn." He looked disgusted. I felt that I ought to apologize for wanting to go there but decided not to, waited silently as he stripped off a white glove and from somewhere in the inner mysteries of his uniform dug out a dog-eared small book with a red paper cover. "How do you spell it?"

"B-R —"

"No! Fur — That street."

"F-U-R-M-A-N."

The cop wet a thumb and started turning frayed pages. "Fairfield," he muttered. "Flatlands. Freedom Square. Here it is, Furman Avenue."

"No," I said. "Furman *Street*."

"Oh! Yeah, there's a Furman Street too. What's the number?"

I glanced at the card. "Four hundred nineteen."

"Yeah. Yeah, I got it. You take the IRT subway. It says here IRT Sub Borough Hall four blocks west."

"I see." But I didn't, not quite. "Does that mean the Borough Hall station is four blocks west of Furman Street or that I walk four blocks west from the station?"

The policeman took off his cap and made a more thorough job of scratching his head. "Hanged if I know." Then he got a sudden inspiration. "I'll look in the front of the book."

"When I went to school," I said wearily, "the answers were in the back of the book. Thanks for your trouble but if it's as complicated as all that I'll take a taxi."

I hailed one, gave the driver the address and climbed in. For the first time that day I felt like smoking. I got my pipe out, tamped into its bowl the mixture that after much experimentation I've found suits me exactly, puffed flame into it.

The bit was comfortable between my teeth and the smoke soothing. I shoved over into a corner, leaned back, stretching out diagonally legs too long to be comfortable in any vehicle. The change of position brought my face into the rear view mirror and, not from any Narcissism but to relax my brain as my body was relaxed, I studied it critically.

There are two things that irk me about that phiz of mine. It is unconscionably young-looking in spite of my twenty-seven years and the staid and serious mien I assume when I can remember the appearance expected of an attorney, even a junior attorney, on the staff of Sturdevant, Hamlin, Mosby and Garfield. Then too, my nose is slightly thickened midway of the bridge, and there is a semicircular scar on my left cheek, mementoes of a certain encounter with a son of Nippon who wielded his Samurai sword a bit too dexterously for my comfort.

Otherwise mine is not too unpleasant a countenance with which to live. I have a thick shock of ruddy brown hair, eyes that almost match it in hue and a squarish jaw I like to think appears strong and determined. I'll never take first prize in a beauty contest, but neither do babes scream at the sight of me. Not even grown-up ones.

Madison Avenue died and was buried in the Square of the same name. We were on Fourth Avenue for a while and then on Lafayette Street. The old Tombs Prison, abandoned now, lifted its formidable granite wall on the left, was succeeded by the white majesty of the government buildings that front Foley Square. The Municipal Building straddled Chambers Street like a modern Colossus of Rhodes and then the blare of City Hall Park was raucous in my ears.

An overalled truck driver disputed the right of way with my cabby. "Where the hell do you think you're goin'?" he wanted to know.

Where did I think I was going? Why did I think I was going towards Evelyn Rand when all the evidence I had of any connection between her and this Achronos Astaris was the faint hint of her perfume on his card?

Evidence? I was a hell of a lawyer! That card need never have been anywhere near Furman Street or Astaris.

Hundreds of them must have been inserted between the leaves of the art gallery's catalogues, and that had been done at the gallery. She'd never been on Furman Street. She had never heard of this Astaris nor he of her.

But the card carried her perfume. I fished it out, lifted it to my nostrils and sniffed. All I smelled was paper and ink.

The fragrance had not, then, come from this bit of pasteboard. But I'd smelled it, I was certain that I had smelled in the street outside that bookstore and again inside. I was a blithering ass. Evelyn had been in that store seconds before I'd entered it. I was running away from, not towards her. "Hey," I yelled to the driver. "Turn around. Turn around fast and go back to where we started from."

"Nix, fella," the cabby grunted. "It's ten days suspension of my license if I turn here on the bridge."

"What bridge?" But staring out of the window I saw that we were on the bridge to Brooklyn and I knew that the ordinance prohibiting a U-turn on it was rigidly enforced. "Okay," I grunted, resignedly. "Guess I've got to wait."

That was the longest, most chafing mile I've ever ridden. The noon rush was just beginning and the roadway was jammed, but at long last the taxi reached the trolley-cluttered plaza at the other end and slowed. "Well," my driver growled at his windshield. "Yuh change your mind again or is it go back?"

"Go on." That wasn't I who'd answered. It was a woman's voice; but so clear, so imperative that the cab's sudden burst of speed thrust me back into my corner and before I'd recovered myself it already was wheeling down a narrow street liberally supplied with one-way arrows.

And with signs that said, TO BOROUGH HALL. Some woman in a car alongside had said 'Go on' to her own driver and somehow her voice had carried to mine. Simple. So simple that in deciding it no longer mattered if I delayed an hour in returning to that bookstore, that I might as well go on and interview Achronos Astaris, I had no sense of yielding to any guidance outside my own will.

And then the driver veered the cab to the curb, braked hard.

"I got a flat, buddy," he turned to inform me, quite unnecessarily, as he heaved out of his seat. "Take me five, six minutes to fix. That's Borough Hall right ahead there. Mebbe if you'd ask a coupla guys where this here Furman Street is while I'm workin' it'll save us time."

"I've got a better idea," I grunted. "I'll pay you off now and walk the rest of the way. According to the cop's book it's only four blocks from here." I, paid him his fare and alighted. If travelling in Brooklyn was a matter of asking questions, I could do that with the best.

Asking questions was one thing, getting informative replies another. In turn a newsstand attendant, a brother attorney hurrying, briefcase in hand, toward the nearby Courthouse and a bearded der- elict standing hopefully beside a little portable shine-box shrugged doubtful shoulders and looked blank. Finally, I approached a policeman with some trepidation. If he produced a little red booklet —

But he didn't. "Furman Street," he said. "That's over on the edge of Brooklyn Heights. Cross this here street and go past that there corner cigar store and keep going and you'll walk right into it."

I heaved a sigh of relief. It was exceedingly premature. My brisk pace slowed as I found myself in a maze of narrow, decorous streets labelled with such curious names as Orange, Cranberry, Pineapple. I entered a still narrower one designated College Place and brought up facing a blank wall that forbade further progress. I extricated myself from that *Cul-de-sac*, walked a little further and halted.

I had lost all sense of direction.

From not far off came the growl of city traffic, the honk of horns, the busy hum of urban life, but all this seemed oddly alien to this street where I was, this street of low, gray-facaded houses with high stone stoops and windows shuttered against prying eyes. Years and the weather had spread over them a dark patina of age yet there was about them a timeless quality, an air of aloofness from the flow of events, from the petty affairs of the very mankind for whose shelter they had been erected. The houses seemed to possess the street so utterly that no one moved along the narrow sidewalks or appeared at the blinded windows, or let his voice be heard.

I was strangely alone in the heart of the city, strangely cloistered in drowsy quiet.

Into that quiet there came a low sonorous hoot, swelling till the air was vibrant with it, fading away. The sound came again and I knew what it was. A steamboat whistle. I recalled that the taxi had not run far from the Bridge, that the East River must be very near. I recalled, too, what the policeman had just said about Furman Street's being on the edge of Brooklyn Heights. It would overlook the River, then, and the direction from which the whistle had come would be the direction in which lay the thoroughfare I sought.

I turned in that direction, saw a drugstore on the nearest corner, and started for it. I'd get straightened out there.

The shop was small, low-ceiled, the shelving and showcases white and very clean. There was no soda fountain. Glass vases filled with colored water, red and green, stood at either end of a high partition.

I heard the clink of a pestle on a wedgewood mortar behind that partition. It stopped when I cleared my throat loudly. A dark green portiere moved aside to open a doorway and the spectacled, white-coated pharmacist came out.

"How do you do?" he greeted me pleasantly, tugging at one drooping wing of a pair of walrus mustaches. "Warm for this time of the year, isn't it?" He came leisurely toward me, smiling.

"I wonder if you can direct me to Furman Street."

"Certainly." The druggist took me by the arm, impelled me gently to the door, opened it. "You haven't far to go, but it makes a difference which number you want. The two hundreds are that way," pointing, "but it's shorter to the four hundreds if you go up Plum Street." He indicated a thoroughfare at an acute angle to the one he'd first gestured to.

"I'd better go up Plum, then," I said. "The number I'm looking for is four-nineteen."

"You must be mistaken, sir. There is no such number on Furman."

I answered his smile with my own. "But there is. I'm positive that is the address." I brought the card out of my overcoat pocket and once more read it. The number was distinctly and indubitably 419. "Look here." I displayed the pasteboard to the pharmacist. "Isn't that 419 Furman Street?"

The druggist looked at the card. Then be looked up at me, and the smile was gone from his face. "Listen, old man." His hand was on my arm, solicitously. "Furman Street is very long and there might be an easier way for you to get to where you want to go than along Plum. Sit down here a minute," he led me to a bentwood chair in front of a showcase, "while I go in back and look up just where four-nineteen is."

I couldn't quite make him out, but he was being so decent to me that I couldn't argue with him. I sat down and watched him hurry back behind the partition to consult, as I supposed, another one of those little red guidebooks.

I was mistaken. I have exceptionally keen hearing and so I caught from behind that mirrored wall something I definitely wasn't supposed to hear. The pharmacist's whisper, suddenly excited: "Tom! Grab that phone and dial Dr. Pierce. I think that fellow out there is the patient that got away from his asylum last night."

Another whisper came back: "How do you figure that?"

"He just asked me for four-nineteen Furman. Four-nineteen, mind you. And he showed me what he said was a card with that number on it. But there wasn't any card in his hand. There was nothing in it at all."

"Certainly sounds like a nut," I heard the other whisper respond. "You go back out there and keep him talking and I'll get Pierce's keepers over here. Here, you better take this gun along in case he gets violent."

That got me out of the chair and out of that store in a rush. I was a block away before I slowed and stopped.

CHAPTER 4
FORMAN STREET

THERE *WAS* A CARD IN my hand. By the evidence of every possible sense I held the card of Achronos Astaris in my hand. A man who seemed sane insisted that hand was empty, but I could feel the card in it, see it, read the name and address printed on it. It was there. I'd found it in the catalogue of the exhibit where Evelyn Rand's portrait hung.

I did not know that. I'd *decided* the card had been between the pages of that pamphlet because it was madness to permit myself to believe that it had been handed to me during a space of time that occupied no time at all, by a man who did not exist.

But if the card itself did not exist!

Here it was between my thumb and fingers, white, crisp, unquestionable. Even if the pharmacist hadn't seen it, others had. The gray bookseller. The policeman on Madison Ave.

Had they? I had dropped it in the bookstore, had bent to pick it up, but the near-sighted dealer in second-hand tomes had said nothing, done nothing, to indicate that he was aware of why I stooped, of what I reached for. Nor, I now recalled, had I shown the card to either officer.

What if I had not? The card was real, couldn't be anything else but real. I had been meant to hear the druggist's whisper, saying that it was not. It was his perverted idea of a joke. The best thing to do about the incident was to forget it. The card *had* to be real. The alternative was —

I dared not put that alternative into words, even in thought. I could test it however, very simply.

I could go to Furman Street and look for number four-nineteen. If it was there, if a man named Achronos Astaris lived there, I was sane.

My skull felt drained, empty, when I reached that decision. I stared about me. I saw a lamppost and a street sign stiffly projecting from it. The sign said, Plum Street. By continuing on the way I was going I would come to Furman Street, in the four hundred block.

I got moving. This street was as deserted as those through which I had come. Yet I had a queer feeling that I was not alone in it, that someone was keeping ahead of me, just ahead, although I could see no one. The sidewalk curved, climbed quite steeply to brightness about a hundred yards before me. I thought I caught a flutter of misty blue up ahead, but when I looked more closely it was gone.

The houses beside me ended and I halted, staring out into the brightness of sky over water, gazing raptly at the mountainous mass that seemed suspended in that brightness.

Stone and steel and glass, across the bustling water each gargantuan tower was separate and distinct, but all were merged in a jagged pyramid that climbed, colossal in beauty, till its topmost pinnacle challenged the sun. Manhattan's skyscrapers.

After awhile my gaze drifted downward to the swirling, cloudlike haze that obscured the bases of the skyscrapers and made it seem as though they hung unsupported in midair.

Strange, I was thinking, that so late in the day the mists still should be heavy on the Bay, and then I realized that the obscurity was neither cloud nor mist and that it lay not on the water but on the nearer shore.

What my unfocussed eyes had diagnosed as vapor I saw now was a low building that faced the end of Plum Street, a low gable-roofed wooden house, white-painted, with a little green lawn before it. A narrow gravel path went up through the lawn to an oaken door that made a dark, semicircle-topped rectangle in the clapboard facade.

One comes upon such relics of a more gracious past in the most unlikely parts of New York. Mostly, though, they are dilapidated, ramshackle, mouldering to ruin. This one seemed perfectly preserved. The pickets of the wrought iron fence around its pocket handkerchief of a lawn were unscarred by rust, its windows obviously were washed and gleaming even if darkened by the blinds pulled down behind their panes.

From the center of the roof a small domed cupola rose and around it ran a narrow, railed balcony.

Recalling something of my school history, I wondered if George Washington had not perhaps stood on that balcony, spyglass to eye, watching General Gates' redcoats filling the barges that would bring them across the river to the Battle of Brooklyn Heights. Perhaps this house had been his headquarters during that momentous encounter. That would explain its preservation.

On either side of it was a four-storied structure of gray stone, each the beginning of a row running off to right and left paralleling the shore. In front of the building to the left — my left — of the gabled wooden house was a tall brown lamp post and the sign on the lamp post read Furman *Street*.

The number painted on the third step of the high stoop of the house behind the lamp post was 415. The number painted on the third stoop of the stone house to the right — my right — of the low white house was 423.

The house between them, the house with the little lawn and the balconied cupola must be, then, Number 419 Furman Street.

As I went across to it some errant breeze lifted a whirl of dust from the asphalt. It accompanied me across the opposite sidewalk and through the gate in the tall fence of wrought iron. It whispered about me as I went up the path and although I felt the gravel crunch under my feet there was no other sound in the hush than the whisper of that tiny whorl of dust.

The high portal, oak darkened by the years to the tone of old leather and to its secret glow, opened smoothly, silently before me. Without hesitation, almost as though I were no longer master of my own movement, I stepped through the aperture into cool dimness.

The door thudded dully behind me. It shut out the city's low murmur, so omnipresent that I had not been aware of it till now it was gone. It was as if a barrier had come between me and the world I knew.

Passing from the bright winter sunshine to this semidarkness, I was temporarily blinded. I halted, a bit bemused, waiting for sight to be restored.

I could make out no detail of the place where I was. I could see only a gray, featureless blur. But I had an impression of spaciousness — of space really. Of a vast, limitless space that by no imaginable means could be confined within the four walls of a house. Of a space that could not be confined within the four points of the compass!

Abruptly my thigh muscles were quivering and the nausea of vertigo was twisting within me! I seemed to be on the brink of a bottomless chasm. If I took another step I would hurtle down, forever down. The impulse seized me to take that step, to hurl myself, plummeting, into that illimitable abyss —

Hold it, Johnny March! I told myself, voicelessly. Hold everything! This is only the hall of an old house. In a moment your pupils will adjust themselves and you will see it — walls papered with the weeping-willow design you've always liked, hooked rugs on a floor of axe-hewn planks, perhaps a graceful balustraded staircase —

Subconsciously I must already have been aware of all this, for the very foyer I described took shape out of the formless blur. The design I remembered from the Early American Exhibit of the Metropolitan Museum patterned the faded walls. Wide planks made the floor, rutted with decades of treading feet and keyed together by tiny double wedges of wood, and their dull sheen was brightened by oval rugs whose colors were still glowing despite the years since patient hands had fashioned them. Directly ahead of me the wide staircase I had imaged rose, gently curving, to obscurity above, its dark rails tenuous and graceful.

"Well," I said, turning to the person who had admitted me. "This is — " I never finished the sentence.

No one was there. No one at all!

Someone had opened the door for me, and no one had passed me, going away from it. But of course whoever it was had slipped out the door, as I entered.

Was Brooklyn inhabited exclusively by practical jokers? This one wasn't going to get away with it. He couldn't have gotten far. I grabbed the doorknob, determined to go after him.

The door didn't open. It was locked! I was locked in!

That was going too far, much too far. I —

A silken rustle behind me twisted me around. I started to say just what I thought of the proceedings — My mouth remained open, the angry words dying unspoken.

Down the stairs from above were coming tiny feet, a froth of lace, a circular billow of foaming lace that could only be the hems of the multitudinous petticoats women wore in the days when this house was built. Then the filmy blue of a wide hoopskirt descended into view, a pointed bodice tight on a waist my hand could span.

I shook my head, trying to shake the cobwebs out of it. What the devil was this?

The crinolined maiden paused on the stairs, a slim white hand to her startled bosom. For a moment the shadow of the ceiling was across her face, and then I saw it, whitely luminous against the dark background of the stairs.

It was the face of Evelyn Rand! The soft red mouth was tight with pain, the gray eyes peering down at me were haunted with a strange dread; but this was the face that had looked out from the portrait on Madison Avenue . . .

"Evelyn!" I cried, leaping forward. My feet struck the bottom step, pounding upward —

And suddenly were motionless.

She wasn't there any longer. She wasn't above me on the stairs. She hadn't retreated, startled by my cry. She had *blinked out,* in the instant it had taken me to get across the floor and three steps up.

Something was left of her. A faint sweetness on the air. The scent of spring. The scent of dreams.

Of dreams. Was I at it again? Had I only dreamed that I saw her?

"Not quite," a low, toneless voice said behind me. "She was not there, but neither did you dream that she was."

I wheeled, my breath caught in my throat.

Just below me at the stairs' foot, vagrant light from somewhere gleaming on the polished scalp of his too-large head, his lashless and disquieting eyes pinpoints of flame in the gloom, was the little man of the art gallery!

CHAPTER 5

THE RIDDLES OF ACHRONOS ASTARIS

MY FINGERS DUG INTO the rail they had grasped to pull me up the stairs. That at least was firm and hard. That at least was real.

"Less real than I," said the little man who twice apparently had materialized out of nothingness. "The staircase exists only as you have conceived it. So do the walls about us and the floor on which you see me stand."

I'd not spoken aloud the thought to which he responded. Was he reading my mind?

"A crude way of phrasing it," he answered that unspoken thought, "but as near the truth as you can comprehend." Damn him! He was laughing at me. I knew he was laughing at me even though his round face with its artificial-seeming skin was as still as a modelled mask. He was — Hold on, John March. You're in that dream again, that confounded dream. What you think you hear him say is just the answer of one part of your mind to the thoughts of another. You no more see this odd human than just now you saw Evelyn Rand —

"Wrong," the little man said. "You saw her, or rather a projection of her that I presented to you in order to ascertain if what I already had observed is a constant of your psyche or an aberration."

I could not be dreaming that. I had no idea of what it meant. "The hell you say," I flung at him to conceal my growing apprehension. "What am I, some kind of guinea pig with which you're experimenting?"

A faint, mocking smile brushed his still lips. Or did it? "Exactly," he murmured.

That enraged me. "Experiment with this," I yelled and leaped down at him, my fist flailing straight for his round, inhuman face —

It whizzed through empty air! My feet pounded on the floor. The little man had vanished —

Sound behind me whirled me around. The fellow was on the staircase, three steps up. He was exactly where I had been, an instant before! But how in the name of reason had he gotten there? He couldn't have passed me, he couldn't possibly have passed me. To get to where he was he would have had to go up the steps at the same time, by the same path, I had plunged down them. Two bodies cannot occupy the same space —

"Matter can be in one place and then in another," he said in the slow, patient way one explains some complex idea to a child, choosing phrases suitable to its limited comprehension, "without ever having been anywhere between. Even you should know that. Or are you not acquainted with the observations on the behavior of electrons that already had been made in your time."

"In my time! What time?"

"The Twentieth Century, as you reckon it." I had the curious feeling that he was speaking of some period in the remote past. "I am certain our researches are correct on that point."

I shook my head. He couldn't be saying that, he just could not. It didn't make sense. With my confused sense of *wrongness* about all this was mingled a sort of baffled exasperation. Damn him! He was coldly amused by my bewilderment.

Queer! No flicker of the muscles in his face, no changing light in his black and piercing eyes, revealed that to me. But I was as aware of his amusement as though he had laughed aloud. Was I too, very dimly, beginning to learn to do without speech? Was I tapping some subtle current of communication that till now I had not even suspected to exist?

"Who are you?" I blurted. "Who the devil are you?"

He was growing tired of this colloquy between us. "If you must think of me by a name, Achronos Astaris will do." He had stopped playing, was coming to the nub of his purpose with me.

"What, John March, is it that has impelled you to forget everything else in your desire to find Evelyn Rand? What is it that makes her a necessity to you, so that without her you are not complete? What is it that has made ambition, the anxiety for preferment, pride in the occupation you chose for your lifework, insignificant compared with the need you feel for her? What force is it that draws you to her with a strength greater than the attraction of gravity, greater than the thirst of the sodium ion for the hydroxyl group it tears even from water? What chemistry of the emotions has governed your actions since she became real to you?"

His eyes, his dreadful, probing eyes, demanded an answer. "I love her," I flung at Astaris. "God help me, I have fallen in love with her."

I had not known it till that moment, had not realized it. But it was true. I *was* in love with the girl for whom I had been searching so long, the girl whom I'd never seen, with whom I had never spoken.

"Ahhh," Achronos Astaris breathed. "I know that the name of your reaction to her is love." For the first time I sensed a wavering in the clear, cold surety of him. "But what, precisely, does that mean?"

I glared at him, anger once more mounting within me. His eyes gripped mine with a hold almost palpable. He was invading the most secret recesses of my being, was stripping naked my very soul.

Melodramatic phrases, but no phrases less turgid would fit.

"It is most puzzling." Did I hear Astaris say that or was I reading his thoughts? "There is something more than physical chemistry, more than biological tropism, involved. It is plain that he has an urge to hold her naked against his nakedness, to merge —"

"Damn you!" I yelled, outraged. "Damn your rotten, prurient mind," and the wrath that exploded in my brain hurled me up the stairs to smash him —

I smashed instead against — nothingness! Against a wall invisible, immaterial, but as impenetrable as though a screen of armor plate had sprung up between me and the little man.

Still so possessed of wrath that I did not apprehend its full enormity, I clubbed at the unseen barrier with my fists. There was no sound of impact, none at all, but my knuckles were bruised and bleeding. I kicked at empty air and saw the toes of shoes buckle against nothing I could see. Exhausted, I put palms against it and felt perdurable nothingness warm as though it were animate flesh, vibrant with some ineluctable life, impenetrable as granite.

And all the time Achronos Astaris watched me with a cold, mildly interested detachment, as some scientist might watch a Siamese fighting fish batter its nose against glass inserted into its aquarium to bar it from the other *Betta* it has marked as its victim.

He sighed now as I hung, panting and weak against the invisible partition. "You learned quite quickly. There is a definite advance in five hundred years."

I stared at him too choked to speak by anger that had not subsided at all.

Oddly, while Astaris was still clear and distinct as he had been, the staircase, the ceiling and the walls were fading again into the gray, shapeless blur out of which they had formed. I glanced down, anger giving way to panic! There was only grayness beneath me, empty grayness! I looked behind. Nothing was behind me but a fearsome gray vacancy. I was enclosed by it, suspended in it. Once more the terror of height possessed me, the vertiginous, heart-stopping awareness of an unfathomable abyss into which I must plunge when Achronos Astaris released me.

For, wheeling again, I had found his eyes upon me, pulsating pinpoints of black flame, and it seemed to me that only those eyes held me where I was. Not the eyes but an impalpable something, a Force unknowable, that merely manifested itself in those eyes as it reached through the infrangible barrier that had frustrated my attack on Astaris, and embraced me.

And those eyes were not only holding me there, suspended. They were dissecting me, not my body but my ego? soul? — the me that is not physical yet lacking which I would not be. Keen, cutting lancets, they were peeling layer after layer from my psyche, searching, searching for something that was there but that they could not find.

Anger they found, and fear, and bewildered awe transcending fear, but that for which they probed they could not find. Gradually they faltered, at a loss. And then I was aware that Astaris had given up his search, that he was sending a message out into the boundless ether, that he was waiting for a reply.

I do not know, even yet, how I knew all this. I know only that for a little while I had the power, and that I was soon to lose it.

"No," the answer came. Not a voice. Not sound at all. Naked thought from an infinite distance. "Send him to us, but you must remain yet awhile."

Astaris did not like that. I was aware he did not, but I was aware also that he would submit. Abruptly fear flared into terror, into such paralyzing, agonized terror that it rocked the very foundations of my mind.

Now! NOW! *Astaris' eyes released me!* Astaris himself was obliterated by an inward swoop of the grayness. It swirled about me, and I was enveloped by a dizzy darkness.

Not darkness! An absence of form, of color, of reality itself. I was falling through nothingness. I was not *falling*. I was caught up in some vast maelstrom. I was whirling through some spaceless, timeless non-existence altogether beyond experience. I was rushing headlong through incalculable distances, distances beyond comprehension, yet I knew myself to be altogether motionless. The Universe had fallen away from me, was somewhere behind me, light centuries behind me. I was beyond life. I was beyond death. I was beyond being itself.

And all about me was the soft, voiceless whisper of swirling dust.

CHAPTER 6

A SKY TOO LOW, A FEAR TOO GREAT

IT ENDED.

The catapulting rush through infinite distances that were not distances at all, the headlong flight that was static as the stars, ended as it had begun; without jar and without transition.

There was solidity beneath my feet. There was vision once more in my eyes. I was John March again and I was back to reality.

Reality? I stood on a slight eminence in the center of a desolate plain across which a jumble of shattered, great boulders stretched to a horizon strangely too near. There was something — incoherent was the word that rose in my mind — in the shape of the rocks, in the dim hues of their fractured surfaces, and their shadows were not black as shadows ought to be, but a grayish purple. They lay in dark pools about the shattered rocks and the light that made them streamed sourceless out of a sky too low for any normal sky.

The sky weighed upon me as a storm sky would, heavy and ominous, but although no star hung in it, no moon nor star, it was lucidly transparent so that I knew no cloud mass made of it the lowering dome it was. And it was informed with a color such as no sky ever has had, an earthy and fathomless brown that seemed innate in the very air.

The brown lucence bathed the plain, wan and shimmering, and it dawned on me that the wrongly shaped rocks marched toward and past me across the plain as though once they had formed endless collonades and anciently had been smashed by some unimaginable cataclysm. And it seemed to me that in the gray-purple shadows of the rocks Things lurked so outrageous in shape that they had crawled into the deepest shadows to hide even from themselves.

Strangest of all, this landscape seemed vaguely familiar.

A sky too low? A sense of imminent threat? I felt, I swear that I felt fingers brush my eyes and in memory I saw a slim, graceful shape and behind it —

This was the vista that momentarily I had seen, or thought I had seen, form out of the dark, amorphous background of the portrait of Evelyn Rand.

My pulses hammered. Evelyn was somewhere in this gaunt and brooding land. As surely as I knew that I was here myself, I knew that somewhere here was the girl I had sought so long, the girl that in the last few terrible minutes — I'd learned I loved. Somewhere, there had been a landmark in the fleeting glimpse I'd had of this land in the art gallery on Madison Avenue. I turned slowly, searching for it.

And found it.

It loomed against the horizon of the strange low sky, an immensity hewn out of some starless night somehow solid. Black as night and as lustreless, it blotted out a full quadrant of the horizon to which I'd turned, a stygian escarpment deeply scarred and awesome in grandeur, and I now saw that the shattered pillars marched to it from every point of the compass and that their final coming together was buried beneath a black detritus of fragments riven from the monument by the same catastrophe that had destroyed them.

Fragments? They were masses huge as houses and myriads of them were piled in that wide, nocturnal tumulus, yet so tremendous was the shape from which they'd been torn that its configuration had been altered only as much as weathering may alter some heroic statue.

A statue it was, vast beyond any concept of vastness, but of what?

Its haunched body, on whose flanks the skin hung in pendulous folds that were mountainsides in themselves, was a beast's. Its legs — the hinder ones miles-long ridges folded under the colossal body, the fore-limbs soaring towers — were an animal's in contour and posture. But the tremendous head was not that of a beast.

Nor was it human.

It was sunk neckless between the figure's shoulders. It was wide-jawed, lean-jowled. The eyes were hooded with a black, scalp-tight hood, yet somehow I was aware of them, aware of the waiting that brooded in them as long as all the centuries that have been and will yet be, the patience endless as Time.

Impossible to describe that stupendous countenance whose very wrinkles were ravines, impossible not to read in its lineaments a knowledge that transcended the inner mysteries of the Universe and probed to where Space itself ceases to exist.

Limned in that face was all Good. And yet —

And yet stupendously below it, where the curve of one sculptured paw rose out of the jumbled shards, was the shattered outline of another figure modelled out of some pinkish and fleshlike stone. This was the representation of a man and he was contorted in unendurable agony, and into him were driven the monstrous claws to pin him down.

Good above, Evil below. Love above, Hate below and the esoteric knowledge in the vast countenance was that in the eternity-long progress of life from its inchoate beginnings to its ultimate goal, Good and Evil, Love and Hate, are one and the same.

How long I stood immobile, scarcely breathing, possessed wholly by that wonder, I shall never know. How long I might have remained in its spell I cannot tell, for abruptly I was torn from it by the rattle of small stones behind me and a deep-chested, ferocious bellow.

I snatched up a fist-size stone as I whirled, saw that the avid roar was not meant for me. Near the base of my mound a man rolled, scrabbling to regain his feet, and a gorilla leaped toward him, would reach him before he could possibly do so.

With some unformed idea of distracting the shaggy brute I let out an incoherent yell and started running across its line of sight. The beast twisted, saw me, bounded not towards me but angling to intercept me; and as I realized that the slope was steeper than I thought, that I could not change direction. I discerned also that he was no beast. A furry pelt was draped across the hairy torso and over its big-thewed shoulder, and his huge calloused hand clutched the wood handle of a flint-beaded axe.

A yard from me, that axe lifted — I flung my stone, and by sheer luck it struck the Stone Age weapon's head squarely, jolted it from the dawn man's grip. But I could not stop my impetuous rush, plunged headlong into him. I got in one blow that might have been the flick of a butterfly's wing for all the effect it had on him, and then his shaggy arms folded me to his barrel chest and constricted, drove the breath out of me, squeezed my ribs. Sight dimmed —

I was on my knees, hanging head down on arms that knuckled the stony ground, and the dark bulk shuddering to lifelessness on the ground here beside me incredibly was the Neanderthal man who'd almost taken my life. *"Ve vous remercier,"* a light, almost musical voice said above me, *"A fond de ma couar je vous remercier."*

It was the man whom the brute had pursued who thanked me for saving his life. He wiped blood from a long and slender poniard with a lacy but tattered kerchief, and his spindly legs were sheathed in long hose of maroon silk laddered by runs. A sort of vest with sleeves wrapped mangy blue velvet about his meagre chest, and the ruffles at his neck and sleeves were ragged and dingy.

He scabbarded his poniard at his belt and bent to me, his sharp featured, predatory countenance anxious, and spoke again in his queer, archaic French which, oddly, I had no difficulty in comprehending. "You are much hurt, my old?"

"No." I let him help me up. "Not much." He seemed to understand my English as well as I did his French, for he looked relieved. "Seems to me it's I who ought to thank you, mister. I'd have been done for if you hadn't sunk that dagger into him."

"But no." Under a wide brimmed hat, its plumes fluttering, his hair was gray but the scar of an old slash gave a permanently raffish twist to his mouth, and his cheeks, blued by stubble, were sunken and emaciated. "It is my life that I owe to you, monsieur, and though it has many times been declared forfeit to the King's justice, I still set upon it a certain value." The sidewise cant of his eyes was slinking and furtive but in them was a certain dark sparkle of gaiety and about his lank, bony figure there was a swaggering devil-be-damnedness altogether intriguing. "If you had not come to my rescue you would not have been in danger so great."

He swept that wide hat from his head and brought it to his breast as he bowed. "I salute you, monsieur. Such clan, such courage I have not often seen in a life perhaps too much filled with episodes that have required them." He returned the hat to his jauntily cocked head. "If I may have the honor of being made acquainted with your name?"

"John March," I told him, somewhat dazed by this ebullience.

"John March. I shall not forget it when once again I set about my *Grant Testamente*. A vilanelle, perhaps, to express my gratitude. I shall —"

"Your *Grant Testamente!*" I blurted. "A vilanelle? Who are you? In the name of all that is holy, *who are you!*"

"There is very little holy about me." A bitter smile twisted the man's thin mouth. "Or so the abbot of Paris would hold. A jailbird, a liar, a thief. A consort of slitpurses and doxies. A picklock, a runagate o'nights and a lack-brained clerk by day. And-". He straightened, and drew pride around him like a cloak. "And a poet of sorts, I hope. My name — for what it is worth — Francois Villon."

"Villon!" I gasped. "You're kidding me. Francois Villon died four hundred years ago."

"No," the man in doublet and hose said. "Villon did not die. His sins overtaking him at last, he was banished from his beloved Paris. He trudged out through the Porte Sainte Jacques, all he possessed on his back and in a starveling packet under his arm. He plodded out on the Orleans road, weary of life, weary unto death. Though the day was breathless, a tiny swirl of dust whispered towards him, and," once more he bowed, "here you find Francis Villon. Not dead. Most assuredly not dead."

"But — " I still could not bring myself to believe him. "But four centuries. It is impossible!"

"Nothing, my friend," interrupted Francois Villon, "is impossible. Least of all in this land where Time — He paused.

"Yes."

"In this Land," he began again, "where Time is not."

"Where Time-! What do you mean?"

"That, my friend, you will learn — too soon." Villon was once more furtive, his eyes sliding away from mine as he said, "Suppose you satisfy the curiosity that is ever a flame burning within me, and burning me. You are from Britain?"

"No," I answered. "From America." I recalled that the Western Hemisphere had just been discovered in his day, that he might not know the name. "From the continent, Columbus discovered —"

"Yes," he cut in. "I know. She has told me of it. The maiden with the hair of honey and the gray eyes that hide laughter and dreams."

I grabbed his arm, my fingers bruising the thin flesh. "You've seen her, talked with her!" I could hardly get the words out. "She is here."

"She is here indeed. I — " He stopped abruptly. He was looking over my shoulder, and his face was suddenly pallid.

"Where is she?" I demanded. "Take me to her."

"No," Villon responded, and his voice was hollow with fear. "I cannot take you to the fair Evelyn. I cannot take you anywhere. For our hosts appear. I had thought to escape them, but they have found me and they have found you, and now there is no longer any hope for us, or for Evelyn Rand, or for that pleasant world into which we were born and which we shall never see again."

The air burst into an infinitude of darting sparks, green and blue and yellow and scarlet. My skin prickled sharply. Somewhere a white orb blazed. It was the hub of the sparks that immediately whirled about it in countless threadlike circles of luminance that merged into a solid shining disk. This drew in upon its dazzling center.

It was no longer light at all but a Shape, a Thing grotesque and weird and incredible, where nothing had been seconds before.

CHAPTER 7

THE EMPTY SHAPE OF A MAN

FRANCOIS VILLON WAS laughing. There was no amusement in his high, thin laugh, but a sort of wild despair and a sort of madness. Mad indeed was that which had materialized out of a whirl of coruscant light and poised now before us.

It was almost all head, three-quarters a huge ovoid head; yellow-gray skin naked of hair drawn tightly over a monstrous skull. Two enormous eyes, lidless and lashless, swam with an oily iridescence. The head's face had no nose, unless two black orifices just below its midpoint were nares. A round, tiny mouth beneath these putative nostrils was innocent of lips or teeth. Where ears should be, two circular areas of skin pulsed as though the brain within momentarily would burst through membranes too frail to restrain it.

The rest, invested by some dark hued, horny integument, was a bulbous torso out of which grew two boneless tentacles each terminated by splayed and writhing branches — caricatures of hands. Legs there must have been also, and feet of sorts, for the apparition stood upright as a man stands.

"*Voila,* John March," Villon chuckled, "he who calls himself Kass."

It was that chuckle, I think, the amazing effrontery of it, that set my thought processes going again. I did not really see this thing, I told myself. I was the victim of a hypnotic illusion induced by the whirling lights and the white blaze at its center. It was not, it could not be real.

I dragged the side of my hand across my eyes, and looked again, and the great head was still there, its bulging eyes fixed upon me. In their gaze was the same hard, impersonal speculation I had so resented in Achronos Astaris. Somehow more dreadful it was now, for Astaris at least had been human, while this . . .

"I am human," Kass broke in. "A million years more human than you." He did not *say* it. The words were within my own mind, a thought perceived, not heard, but it must have come from him. I could not have formulated it.

Moreover, Villon heard the soundless message too. "A million years more human than you or I," he drawled to prove it, his accents slurred. "Look well, my friend. See to what all mankind's aspirations, all mankind's strivings, shall bring us in the end." My gaze shifted to him. A sardonic grin twisted those thin, scarred lips of his. "In truth there must be a God, for only God could play so bitter a jest."

What they were saying seemed so much grim nonsense, but before I had time to react to it I became aware that Kass's attention had swung to Villon, and I sensed that Kass was puzzled. Once more I was reminded of Astaris, of how when the strange little man had demanded from me the meaning of love I had felt him to be troubled by some queer urgency, by some driving need for a knowledge that was denied him.

"Why do you not fear me?" Kass was inquiring of the Frenchman. "There is the consciousness of utter defeat in you, and despair, but you do not fear me. Why?"

"Fear you?" Villon murmured, insolence in the cant of his narrow head, divine contempt in the stance of the scrawny frame on whose bony angles hung his tattered finery. "I? Who have made a ballade of love's betrayal and a villanelle of torture's rack? Who have metered a rondeau by the clatter of my best friend's bones swung from a gibbet, and flung a roundelay to the rabble with the hangman's knot under my own left ear? Fear you? I who have listened to the music of the Universe and dreamed the dreams of the angels and the damned?

"There is that within me Lucifer cannot touch, nor the God your existence blasphemes destroy. I have gone up into a Heaven of my own devising and down into a Hell of my own imagining, and you can show me no terrors I have not known aforetime. Fear you? I am a poet."

He slapped the face of Kass with his mocking laugh, and there was a hush that was not of sound alone. Or there may have been some reply, but I did not know of it, for in that instant the corner of my eye caught furtive movement among the rocks and my look slid to it, my head not turning.

I glimpsed them only for an eye-blink before the shadows hid them, but in that split-second I saw them clearly and I knew I could not be mistaken, though reason insisted I must be. Reason, even with the animate, tangible presence of Francois Villon to confute it, insisted I could not have seen a knight in chain mail and a forester in the brilliant green of Sherwood Forest peering from behind a boulder's jagged edge, gesturing to me not to betray them.

I did something then that until that moment I should not have dreamed either possible or necessary. I deliberately blotted what I'd seen out of my consciousness, made myself think of something else at once; of the way the pallid and sourceless light glimmered on the round of Kass's skull, of how his monstrous shadow was a grayish-purple like no shadow I had elsewhere seen.

And I did this just in time, for once more he was reading me.

"Matters stranger to you than the color of a shadow there will be to wonder at," he remarked, "before we are prepared to deal with you." It is difficult to convey the feeling of — nakedness — given one by the realization that one's thoughts are exposed to another. "Come. The Council awaits me."

"Lead on, fellow," I said, trying to get jauntiness into my tone. Villon had set me an example of courage I was ashamed not to emulate. "Whither thou goest I shall go." I rather suspected I wouldn't be very successful if I objected, and, too, I had a pretty good hunch that wherever he wanted to take me would bring me nearer Evelyn Rand.

No. All this weirdness into which I had been plunged had not driven the thought of her from my mind. Rather it had multiplied many times my anxiety for her. If she were here, and in the power of creatures like this . . .

A stinging prickle netted my body. Kass's fingers were touching my shoulder; his other hand gripped Villon. "Come!" It was as if abruptly I was at the heart of a maelstrom of some electric force. Panic struck at me. I had felt this same sensation at the moment the grotesque being appeared. Was I about to dissolve into a whirl of flashing, multi-colored sparks?

Nothing happened. Nothing except that the rocks about, the ground beneath, abruptly were flowing past us. We were motionless. It was the plain, the horizon, that moved. A sharp, twanging sound came from my left. Kass's touch was gone and the speeding earth pulled my feet from beneath me. I pitched forward headlong. Falling, I twisted, saw the writhing fingers that had released me pluck something from the air. A feathered arrow!

My shoulder hit the now motionless dirt. "Up, *St. George!*" a deep-chested voice bellowed, metal rattling through it. "Have at thee, hell spawn!" The burly, mailed figure I had glimpsed lunged out from behind a rock, his linked gauntlets sweeping a great two-handed sword down upon our captor's sickly-hued, immense skull. "Die, caitiff!" someone else cried, and a lithe green figure leaped past Villon, also fallen, and thrust a dagger at Kass's great eye.

The knight's broadsword shattered into a thousand clanging shards; the forester's knife, arrested in blank air, shivered as though it had jabbed into the trunk of an oak.

Neither blade had touched Kass, though the latter had not moved by the tenth of an inch. No one was moving now. All the fierce motion had stopped; the pounce of the ambushers from the covert which the flow of the landscape had brought to us, the skid of our momentum that had taken Villon and myself yards along the suddenly halted ground.

The scene held. Kass; one tentacle lifted to grasp the arrow, the membranes at either side of his gargantuan eyes a trifle distended, no other sign of emotion about him. The knight; bladeless hilt clutched in chain-gloved fists, longskirted cloak of iron mesh enveloping columnar legs straddled to give foundation to his futile blow, all his head but his swarthy, hate-darkened face swathed in metal fabric, all his immense strength impotent. The other, the forester —

He was a lithe and slender arc, fluid movement abruptly rigid. His shoes, of some soft, chamoislike leather and pointed of toe, were green. His taut legs were tightly sheathed to the waist in the emerald of May leaves and his sleeveless leather jerkin repeated the hue as did the fabric that puffed about his shoulders and enveloped his extended arm, thrusting a dagger into the nothingness that held it. In spite of a flame-colored beard his countenance was youthful and debonair, though contorted now by a furious despair. The green, conical hat he wore sported a cocky, crimson feather.

Curious how one's mind works sometimes. There was in mine at that instant, not disappointment at the failure of the ambush I had anticipated and done my best not to betray, not consternation at the manner in which Kass had defeated it, but only a sort of dazed amazement at the anachronistic assembling of the figures in that strange tableau.

The cut of his coat of mail dated the sword-wielder as from the twelfth century. It was in the fourteenth that the Lincolnshire lads prowled Sherwood Forest attired in the green the forester wore. Francois Villon's Paris was that of the fifteen hundreds, and I — my birth date was the year nineteen hundred and twenty. Kass aside, we represented eight centuries of history. Eight hundred years! Absurd! They were masqueraders —

What of the Dawn Man I had fought and Villon had slain? That slavering brute had been no actor. Abruptly I was cold with recollection of the Frenchman's words: "Nothing, my friend, is impossible in this Land Where Time is Not," and then I was cold with something more imminent; a sound, a toneless squeal so shrill that it was at the upper threshold of hearing, a high, thin whine that pierced my ears and set my teeth on edge. It came from the tiny, puckered mouth that seemed so ludicrously inept in the vast yeasty expanse of Kass's visage and it was the first actual sound I had heard him utter.

It went on and on like a wire pulling through my brain, a blue fine wire that was all edge, all wounding edge. It flickered out into the dull, desolate glow brooding over that plain of tumbled rock and ominous shadows, and somewhere out there it found a response. Somewhere from among the malformed boulders, from among the gray-purple shadows that lurked at their bases and filled the mouths of their caves with mystery, *something* was answering Kass.

I rolled, tried to find the source of that second thin whine. My straining eyes could discover nothing alive in all that dreary tumulus. I saw only vacant chaos, only the gaping empty maws of caverns filled by impenetrable shadows.

The shadows were lengthening. That was queer, here where there was no sun to lower; then I realized that only one of the shadows was lengthening. It was flowing like a dark cloud, out of the mouth of a nearby cave. Like a gray-purple fog that somehow had more substance than a fog, it still was formless as drifting mist.

"*Pater Noster in excelsis . . .* " I heard Villon mumble a Latin prayer. And then I heard him gasp, "A drina. God preserve us! I thought they were chained to their lairs by the light."

The cloud parted from the shadow and was a shapeless blob about the size of a small auto, moving more and more swiftly toward us. The tenuous whine that answered Kass's call came from it. It was animate with a blind and groping sort of life, yet it had no shape. Or rather its shape was constantly changing as it billowed toward us, as once in a microscope I had seen the outlines of an amoeba change. Because of this it had no identity, but individuality it had in full measure, and a terrible malevolence.

Kass's call rose shriller. The approach of that purple-gray mass grew swifter, and something in the sightless way it moved made me more certain that were it not for the strange sound Kass made it would not have appeared, and having appeared would not know which way to move. I could see it more clearly, could see now that near its center there was a throbbing spot of deeper purple that did not change in shape, and I was afraid.

I was deathly afraid of the thing Villon had called a *drina*. I was afraid of it because, for all its formlessness, for all its blindness, I sensed intelligence within it, and I knew that intelligence was different in some terrible way from the intelligence of any creature I'd ever known.

Its shrill whine had an eager sound now. It rushed past me and two heart-stopping screams twisted me about!

Knight and forester hung high above the ground, each wrapped around the waist by one of Kass's pipestem tentacles. They were puppets with jerking, boneless limbs, with white masks on which the features had been ineptly splotched, so little of human had terror left in them. The drina boiled toward them.

Kass flung them down and the gray-purple mass rolled over them. Rolled over them and — rolled past where they'd fallen, and they were no longer there.

I saw them! I saw them sprawled within that monstrous purple bulk, forms blurred and indistinct like shapes seen in a pea-soup fog — and *still alive!* Still moving. And then, as the pitch of Kass's squeal changed, *I saw them melt.*

The drina was scudding away towards the nearest shadow-pool, reached it, merged with it. It was gone, and mailed knight and green-clad forester were gone, and there was only Kass, poised here, motionless and silent now, to all appearances already oblivious to what had occurred.

On the ground between him and the cave into which the drina had vanished lay the bladeless hilt of a two-handed sword, a dagger, and a heap of iron links that still retained the empty shape of a man. That was all . . .

Not quite. A little farther away, caught on jagged stone, a conical green hood flaunted a cocky, crimson feather.

CHAPTER 8

ADALON, CITY OF DREAD

"THEY WERE FOOLS," I heard Villon murmur. "But they were brave fools. May God rest their troubled souls."

"Amen!" I managed to say.

Kass was gesturing for us to rise. I shoved shaking hands against the ground to obey, but I was sick, mentally and physically sick. I must have looked it, for the Frenchman, misunderstanding, said as he rose lithely. "There is nothing for you to fear, my friend. Not, at least, till you have served the purpose for which they have brought you here, or until, like those whose passing we have just looked upon, they have found you useless for that purpose."

"They!" I snapped. "Who are they? And what do they want from me?"

"He is one of them," Villon answered, nodding at the approaching Kass, "and the others are as like him as I am like you. They say they are men, as you have heard, and they say that between them and us stretches a million years and more of time. How that can be I do not know, yet neither do I know how it can be that we two are met, living, and nearly of an age though four centuries divide our natal days. If this smaller miracle can come to pass, why not the greater?"

Before I could answer that Kass reached us and laid his splayed hands on our shoulders. At once my body was again stung with countless prickles, and the landscape was once more moving past us.

It accelerated rapidly till the plain and the rocks and the sky itself became nothing but a streaked, brownish blur whizzing past us. We were not moving at all, it was everything outside of us that moved. I felt not the slightest intimation of that inner awareness of motion that the psychologists call the kinesthetic sense. There was nothing around me, nothing to protect me, yet there was no wind on my face . . . Wind! At this unguessable speed the air should have been a solid thing, driving the breath from my lungs, tearing the clothes from my back.

It was, I thought, as if somehow we were detached from the Earth and it were spinning beneath us.

"You are not upon Earth at all," Kass's soundless voice told me. "You are no longer in its space nor of its time."

"What do you mean?" I yelled. "What in hell do you mean?" I shouted because I was frightened, because I was desperately afraid — and hated myself for it.

"It shall be explained to you, if the Council so decides." Kass seemed to be coldly interested in my agitation, in the way I might have been interested, watching a puppy growl at its image in a mirror. "You have, in what you already know, a foundation for comprehension of the matter such as is possessed by none of the others Astaris has sent us, except one. The female from your own generation."

The female! Did he mean Evelyn? The landscape about us was slowing! I made out that we were in a narrow, rugged ravine whose rocky walls were speeding past us.

Then these were gone, and there was no longer any motion.

Some five hundred yards behind us was the towering tumulus that had sped past us. Between it and us stretched a plain level and uncluttered as a concrete highway at dawn.

Ahead, and too close for comfort, the ground dropped sharply down as at the edge of a precipice and I was staring across miles of sheer vacancy to another plateau. There was a shimmering, dream-like quality about this, an appearance, I discerned, due to my seeing it through a peculiar quiver of the air that rose from the curving edge of the chasm to the low, brooding sky. Like a vast, transparent curtain this was, intangible yet very real.

"Down, my friend," the Frenchman said softly. "Look down."

I stepped a little nearer the verge of the cliff. I looked down — a thousand feet, two thousand! I saw nothing but rock, gently curving inward, glass-smooth rock glimmering with high polish. My sight slid down another thousand feet and another, to where that astounding wall curved inward and levelled out to become the bottom of a vast bowl, a mile deep and five miles, I was to learn, across the diameter of its circling rim.

I have mentioned once, I think, the effect of height upon me. Now the illness seized me; my stomach went plummeting down into that yawning gulf. My muscles lost all strength. I toppled forward over the brink of that awful precipice . . . I did not fall. I hung, arms sprawled out, a scream choked in my throat, my skin clammy with the sweat of terror. I hung above that sheer and terrible drop, and I was sustained by nothing I could feel or see.

Kass did not seem to notice but Villon pulled me back and stood me erect on legs gone rubbery, and he smiled at me and said, "You could not fall, my friend."

Our captor's bulging eyes were unfocussed, he was motionless as if absorbed in some weird voiceless communication with someone I could not see. I pulled in breath. "What do you mean, I could not fall?"

"The Veil of Ishlak," Villon gestured to the shimmering curtain that was no more substantial than the quiver of heated air above a railroad track in midsummer, "will not permit you to. So look down without fear, my friend, upon the city of Adalon while yet there is time for you to see what manner of place it is to which your fate has brought you."

I gritted my teeth and peered over that brink once more. Nausea still made me most unhappy, but because I knew now that I could not fall, the vertigo did not blind me. I took it by easy stages, let my eyes drift slowly down along that infernal wall.

My first impression of its smoothness was confirmed. The contour of the precipice was utterly regular, too regular to be natural. This abysmal pit had been quarried out of the solid rock — not quarried. There were no marks of tools or blasting. It seemed, rather, that the huge depression had been hollowed out by a heat so great that the unwanted stone had boiled into vapor and steamed away.

That was, of course, manifestly impossible, but how otherwise the formation could be explained I did not know. My gaze reached the level floor of the bowl. I saw the city of Adalon, dwarfed by height and laid out for me like a map.

Its structures were of the same color and texture as the rock, as though they had not been built but had grown or been moulded out of it. They were square and squat and ugly and no attempt at beautification, no thought of anything but utility, was evident in their design.

One, at the very center of the circular area, dominated all the rest by reason of its vastly greater size, and differed from them also in having a domed roof instead of a flat one. There were eleven other buildings. They were of varying sizes and they were scattered about the bowl's floor at varying distance from the hub, yet I had a curious sense that they were located according to some definite plan, and that the plan had some meaning for me.

"Like a sow and its rooting piglets," Villon murmured, "are they not? And see, some of the piglets themselves have their own offspring clinging close."

"Yes." Except for the central building and the two nearest it, each of the structures of Adalon had other smaller ones very near to it. The third had only one, the fourth two, but there were nine about the fifth.

The sixth also had nine — but these were connected by a wide-topped circular wall in which they were embedded like scattered stones in a ring. "Saturn," I exclaimed. "The ringed planet. The planet with nine satellites and a ring." Now I knew what Adalon's design represented. "The biggest building at the center is the Sun. Mercury, nearest it, and Venus, have no satellites. The Earth, third away, has one moon, Mars has two, and Jupiter nine. It works out, by George, it works out. The three the other side of Saturn would be Uranus and Neptune and Pluto. Don't you see it, Villon? They've built their city in the pattern of the Solar System, of the Sun and its planets."

He looked at me rather queerly. "The Sun and its planets," he whispered. "Aye, it seems to me that once I heard the rector of the university prate of this Mercury and Venus and Mars whereof you speak, and Jupiter too, as stars in the sky of nights, though those other names are strange to me. The Sun and its planets," he repeated. "Now is there some meaning here? I have wondered why they builded thus, higgledy-piggledy, when all else they do has a straight design serving its purpose and no more."

There were little flecks of light between his drooping lids. "Can it be," he whispered. "Can it be that these men a million years older than us, to whom love and beauty and even awe of their Creator are things forgotten and unknown, have yet some sentiment left? A nostalgia, perchance, for the skies they have forsaken, for the orbs that gave them birth?"

He had some other thought, some thought he was as carefully blotting out of his consciousness as I had blotted from mine the thought of the ambush that had failed so disastrously, and for the same reason. But what he had said was enough to make me grab his arm, my fingers digging in.

"Look here," I demanded. "Don't tell me you've swallowed all that stuff Kass has been spilling. That this isn't the Earth, and they're men of the future, and the rest of it."

Villon shrugged, expression draining from his narrow countenance. "It is what they say and they do not lie. There is much about them I do not know, but of one thing I am certain. To the Ishlak in nothing is sacred save the Truth, and the Truth to them is Divine."

I almost believed it all, in that moment I almost believed that Kass and the others who had built Adalon were men of a million years from my own time, that this strange place was not on Earth, that it was beyond the Solar System, perhaps beyond even our Galaxy. But not quite. It was too much to ask a man to believe, too much to ask him to conceive. All that one has been taught cannot be discarded in a single hour no matter how crowded that hour has been with happenings that seem to controvert the very essentials of one's philosophy.

Or was it an hour? Was it not years, a timeless time, since I'd walked along a Brooklyn street — "Listen, Villon," I exclaimed, recalling why I'd walked along that street. "Twice you've mentioned Evelyn Rand. Was it down there that you met her?"

"Aye," he replied and the sparkle was back in those black eyes of his. "She brightened that city of dread so that one did not quite so much miss the sun."

"Okay," I growled, my pulses pounding. "If she's in it, city of dread or no I'm going down there."

"Yes" Villon sighed. "I think you are." He pointed a long finger down to the dome of the central structure, and in that great hemi-spherical roof a hole was opening, irislike. "I doubt me that you will like much what you find there, yet I would give my hopes of salvation, such as they are, if I were awaited as you are in Adalon."

CHAPTER 9

'MORE MERCIFUL IS THE GALLOWS' DROP'

A SILVERY SOMETHING leaped out of the aperture of the roof of the structure I'd likened to the Sun. It shot, on a long, steep slant, straight for us, and so fast was its flight I could see nothing of it but blurred light streaking the air.

In the next instant it was hanging before me, absolutely motionless, in midair. Long axis horizontal, it was cylindrical, one end blunt-tapered like the nose of a bullet, the other square-cut. It was nine or ten feet long, about five in diameter. It seemed to be made of some metal that was a little grayer than silver, and it hovered there without visible support of any kind.

The only man-made things I know of that might approximate this feat are the balloon and the helicopter. No balloon could have moved with anything like the speed this had, nor could one have been brought to a standstill with such abruptness. It was no helicopter either. It had no whirling windmill vanes. In fact, I could make out no protruding part of any kind. The thing simply and unequivocally defied gravity.

I had just about time to note this and to become aware of a curious whirr that seemed to come from the object, when at its nose there was a quick succession of crimson sparks. At once I heard a long, ripping sound, like silk tearing.

"The Veil has parted," Villon answered my startled look, gesturing to a still place in the curtain of shimmer, like an oil slick on water. The projectile leaped inward, hissed along the ground, was static again beside Kass, who seemed to be rousing from his absorption. The whirr cut off.

"They call it a *stratcar*," the Frenchman told me. "I went to my knees in prayer when first one sprang upon me." Impish amusement danced in his eyes, and he chuckled. "I was persuaded that Lucifer in very person had arrived in it to claim my soul, so many times over forfeit to him."

A pale inner glow wavered over the surface of that about which he spoke, like waves of luminosity fluctuating over the surface of superheated steel, yet within a long stride of it I felt no heat. A white line was stripping along its side, from truncated rear to where the taper of its prow began.

"The magic art," Villon's chatter continued, "by which they cause the ground itself to flow past them, miles in a twinkling, appears to fail them at the brink of this chasm. To reach their Adalon from here they fly down to it in this iron contrivance. They fly, mark you. Now this indeed fills me with doubt of my senses, for while magic is a proper matter recognized by all theologians and metaphysicians, for a man to build an engine that flies, goes against Nature. Yet I swear to you, my John, that this stratcar is no uncouth bird but a thing wrought out of metal."

The line that slashed the side of it was widening. The upper half of the stratcar's curved skin was sliding up and around. From within it, toward the front, projected the big head and bulbous upper body of a goggle-eyed individual who might be Kass's twin except that the hard-looking stuff covering his torso was a brilliant orange instead of the dark brown that clothed the other.

Kass's tentacles lifted in what was evidently a salute. The newcomer imitated him, perfunctorily. Then I realized that they were conversing, though I heard nothing, aurally or within my skull.

"Kass seems pretty damned respectful to this new goon," I remarked. "Who is he? Mayor of Adalon?"

"He calls himself Daster," Villon replied. I thought I detected a puzzled note in his voice, and his eyes were narrowed. "The hue of his singlet marks him as a *Doctil*, as that of Kass tells that he is a *Plebo*. Daster is one of the *Kintat*, the Council of Five who rule this land, and that he should come to meet us is passing strange. Does it mean that something has occurred to change the even tenor of their ways during my witless attempt at escape from them?"

I had already begun to suspect that the membranes at the sides of the heads of the Adalonians were their sole features that might be said to have expression. Those of both were vibrating rapidly, seeming to confirm the poet's idea that they were disturbed.

Their colloquy ended, Kass swung to us. "Go," he commanded. "Into the stratcar."

Villon shrugged. "It appears that you are to have your wish, John." He started for the strange vehicle and I followed him. I can't say that I was very comfortable at that particular moment. I didn't like being ordered around, for one thing. And for another, Villon's warnings had convinced me that some very unpleasant experiences were waiting for me in the place to which I was about to be taken.

But Evelyn Rand was down there. There were two seats inside the stratcar, very much like those of an auto. Daster occupied the front one. I got into that in the rear, alongside Villon. I was surprised that the conveyance did not roll as I pressed down on its side, climbing in. It should have, balanced as it was on its rounded bottom. It certainly should have. But it was rigid as though that bottom lay flat against the ground.

I turned to see what would hold it steady when Kass got in, but he did not. His tentacles lifted in repetition of the salute with which he'd greeted Daster. The latter answered him, and then the Plebo was moving away. We were moving away from him, rather, though in relation to the ground we were not moving at all. The mouth of the ravine across the plain swallowed him.

"Didn't he say that the Council was waiting for him?" I exclaimed.

"Yes," Villon breathed. "And that too is strange, for they do not easily chanore their plans. Something indeed is not as it should be in Adalon. Has it any meaning for us? Dare we hope-?" he cut off, and I knew that once more he was veiling his thoughts.

Ignoring us, Daster reached forward to a bank of buttons on the back of the stratcar's nose, that was a circle-edged wall before him. The vehicle's side-wall slid tip from beyond Villon, slid over and came down on my side. We were at once in absolute darkness, a blackness that seemed to thumb my eyes with palpable weight.

The lightlessness lasted only a second. Daster's grotesque head was silhouetted against a greenish, spectral glow. The wall in front of him had become a luminous screen on which, about the level of my chest, rows of buttons were spots of scarlet. Above these, vague blurs took form, became a picture in grays and blacks of the plain outside, the high, rocky cliff that edged it.

They have radar, I thought. But this is more highly developed than any I know.

The Doctil touched another button. The stratcar filled with the whirr I had heard as it hung in midair. Villon gasped and caught at my arm, his fingers digging in.

The whole structure within which we were enclosed was vibrating in correspondence with that whirr. I was thrown to the right, hard against the carside, and Villon against my own left side. The photolike scene on the screen was whisking to the right and I realized that the stratcar was spinning around to point at the Veil through which it had come.

The pressure against my sides eased. The screened image was steady again. Past Daster's head it photoed space and beyond it the distant rim of the bowl within which Adalon lay. My ears seemed stuffed with that infernal whirring. It rose in pitch and I was forced against the back of the seat. Blankness flashed over the screen . . . was replaced at once by a picture of a vast, glass-smooth, curved precipice leaning precariously toward us . . . shifting into a view of the bowl bottom lifted in a disturbing slant so that the buildings seemed about to slide off it.

Those buildings ballooned in size with breathtaking swiftness. It was we who were catapulting down to them, of course, with heart-stopping speed. The acceleration was a weight crushing me against the seat-back, crushing in my chest. Pluto flicked off the screen-edge. Uranus. Saturn. The screen showed only the immense rounded dome of the House of the Sun, a lustrous convexity against which we were going to smash!

A black splotch spotted the exact center of that roof-image, widened to swallow it. I could breathe again. I was no longer crushed in my seat. The whirr had ended. Light was coming into the stratcar, a bar of daylight cutting horizontally across the right hand wall, and widening rapidly. A bar of white sunlight, not the drab, oppressive glow out of which we had just come.

The stratcar's upper half slid over and down beyond my seatmate. The poet's eyes were closed. He had slumped, motionless and limp.

I grabbed for his shoulder. "Villon," I exclaimed. If something had happened to him . . . "Francois!" I realized how much his indomitable cheerfulness, his insouciance, had endeared him to me in the short time I'd known him. If I was still sane it was because of his jauntiness, his gay fatalism.

His eyelids fluttered open and a rueful grimace twisted his mockina lips. "Thus one must fall," he murmured, "when the gibbet trap is sprung from beneath one's feet. But at the end of that drop is at least oblivion, provided the executioner has rightly knotted his noose. Aye, more merciful is the gallows' drop than that which awaits us."

"You've got hanging on your mind a devil of a lot," I snapped.

"And so would you, my John," he grinned wanly, "if you had been condemned to hang as often as I have been."

I twisted to a touch on my shoulder. It was Daster's splayed hand. He had climbed out of the stratcar and he wanted me to do the same. We were in a barnlike room, its floor apparently of the same fused and congealed rock that formed the sides of the bowl. The illumination was not sunlight but came from a wide, shining band circling the walls just where the domed ceiling rested on them, walls that lacked any sign of door or window.

Our stratcar was one of many that stood in a straight row across the chamber. Three Adalonians were clustered about a machine whose nose had been stripped of its metal covering to reveal an intricate mass of gears that they seemed to be repairing. They were, judging by the brown of their torso covering, Plebos, but an orange-clad Doctil was coming toward us.

He reached us as I dismounted from the stratcar. "Gohret," Daster greeted him, lifting his tentacles in salute. "This is John March, whom Astaris' last message concerned."

Gohret's great eyes rested on me very briefly, shifted to Villon who by now stood beside me. "And the other, of course, is the one who was lately found missing," he remarked. "I understand that the scanners located him near the entrance whorl."

"Exactly," Daster agreed. "And so Kass was able to pick up both at once and bring them to the brink together."

"Have you determined how this Villon succeeded in penetrating the Veil of Ishlak?"

"No. Kass reported that he evidently has learned how to conceal his thoughts from us. We shall have to probe his mind in the observation cell."

"Which must be done at once. We must find and punish the Plebo who assisted him. If it was a Plebo." Seeing the two together in that bright light I realized that there was a definite variance in their appearance, difficult to describe but differentiating them sufficiently for recognition. "I shall take charge of him and have the matter attended to immediately."

It seemed to me that Daster resented Gohret's dictatorial tone, but he said nothing to confirm this impression. "Come along," Gohret commanded Villon. "Unless you wish to tell us now that which we want to know."

Francois' lip curled scornfully. "I am too experienced a jailbird to be frightened into blabbing by hints of torture."

"We are not compelled to resort to torture," Gohret responded, "to obtain information we desire. Our methods are more — efficient."

Villon winced. In spite of your pretty speech about a poet and fear, I thought, you're scared, my friend. Hellish scared. That's because you don't know what they're going to do to you and that excellent imagination of yours is working overtime.

"Come along," Gohret commanded again, reaching a long tentacle for Francois. The latter shrank back against the stratcar and the Doctil's writhing limb wrapped around him. Villon's mouth gaped in a soundless scream as agony grayed his face. I swung a fist at the Adalonian. Its knuckles sank into squashy, rot-soft flesh under Gohret's tiny mouth and my other fist, driving in, was caught in midair as Daster's arms roped me, lifted me from the floor. I kicked back at him, furiously. My heels crunched. Pain rayed through me, traced every nerve in my body.

I hung from those terrible tentacles, paralyzed, halfblinded and, inconsequently, resenting it that the Plebos had not even turned from their work to watch me fight.

"Thank you, my friend," Villon called, his voice thin with his own agony. "You meant well but you could have done me no good, no good at all." Gohret's tentacle grooved the poet's scrawny chest and on the back of Villon's dangling hand blood trickled from the crushed flesh of his arm. "You cannot help me." They were sinking, visibly they were sinking into the floor and unless I was mistaken — I must be mistaken — the floor rose along their bodies undisturbed.

"Farewell, John March." He was smiling. He actually was smiling up at me, the indomitable fellow, only his shoulders and his head and his plumed hat still visible. "Tell the fair Evelyn that though I go now into eternal darkness I take with me the recollection of the gray-eyed Angel I met in Hell."

CHAPTER 10

SOME INCREDIBLE OTHERWHERE

THE FLOOR WAS solid over where Francois Villon had vanished. Daster set me down and the power of my muscles returned and the agony of my nerves faded.

I was alone in that stratcar hangar now with those strange beings that were so unhuman in appearance and yet so oddly human. I was alone and, I admit it without shame, I was afraid.

It was my turn, now, to be punished. For striking Gohret. For kicking at Daster. I faced around to the remaining Doctil, doing my best to stand straight, forcing myself to look into his mucid eyes. They were coldly impersonal. They lay upon me for what seemed a long time, altogether without emotion. Astaris had looked at me like that, and Kass, and slow resentment welled up in me again at the sense of inferiority that steady, speculative gaze inflicted upon me.

Daster's arm lifted in a gesture, and I knew I was to go with him — somewhere.

We started moving across the hangar floor, myself a little ahead. The Plebos to one side busied themselves with their task, not for one instant interrupted.

Where was I being taken? We were walking directly towards the opposite wall of that vaulted chamber, and there was nothing there but the blind face of the stone. It was so highly polished that it reflected us, vaguely. There was no seam where it rounded into the floor. Floor and wall and dome were of one piece, like concrete that had been formed in a mould. But they were not concrete. They were rock. How could rock have been poured that way?

"All things are plastic," Daster answered me, "at some degree of heat."

"True enough." Aeons ago, I recalled from my geology, the Earth itself was molten, shaped into an orb by the very speed of its spinning, bulging at the equator because there the centrifugal force was the greatest. "But the heat that melts rock is so great that it would be impossible for men to shape it, in such large masses at any rate."

"Nothing," the Doctil answered, "is impossible to man."

"You-!" I stopped short. I was face to face with my reflection in the wall, another half-step would bring me against it.

"Go on, John March." His hand on my back shoved me forward, gently. I went into that rock . . . *Not against* it, *into* it! It impeded me no more than so much air, but for a moment I was blinded by intangible grayness. Then there was light again and I was in a narrow corridor that spiralled downward, the pitch so steep that I had to lean back and dig heels to keep myself from going too fast.

"What — what the devil!" I couldn't help the exclamation. "How did that happen?"

"Matter is not really solid," Daster answered, "as you should know, but is composed of vibrating electrons separated by spaces compared to which their own sizes are minute. The rate of vibration of the wall rock has been adjusted so that the electrons of which we are composed may flow through, *between* its particles."

"It's as simple as all that, is it?" I tried to be sarcastic. "Good thing the boys in Sing Sing don't know about it or they'd walk out some fine morning."

"Precisely. Except that the technique of changing the vibration rate of the prison walls would have been beyond the ability of even the most profound scientists of your time. That was not developed until some five hundred years after your period."

"Oh yeah?" I wasn't going to let myself be worked up again by the way these people kept tossing the centuries about, regardless. "Just a little matter of five hundred years." If I let myself believe that time had folded into itself, Daster and his friends might really be a million years beyond me in evolution. The inevitable implication of that would be that I was up against people I could have no hope of fighting. And I wasn't ready to admit that, not quite yet. "Just the day after tomorrow to you."

"No," Daster dissented, dryly. "The day before yesterday."

Now what could I do about that except shut up? We kept on going down and around, and though my own footfalls echoed within the confines of that interminable spiral, the Adalonian's movements were soundless. A Latin tag came out of my high school *days — facile descensus Averni,* greasy is the descent to Hades — and the speculation trailed across my mind that perhaps I had died in that old house on Brooklyn Heights; that, a disembodied soul, I wandered through some Afterland beyond death.

Abruptly the passage leveled out under my feet, straightened out. Far ahead there was a tiny oblong of the same curiously brownish light that had pervaded the plain above. It grew larger swiftly, although I was walking at an ordinary pace. I realized that all this time my footing had been moving, without vibration, an endless belt spiralling down from that lofty stratcar hangar.

The rectangle of light ahead became a squared opening at which the tunnel ended. I was through it, Daster's touch on my elbow keeping me from falling as I left the conveyor. I half-spun, saw that

I'd emerged from an aperture in a blue-gray wall, lifted my look and saw that wall towering, windowless, tremendously above me.

So great was its height that it appeared to lean appallingly forward, to be about to hurtle down upon me. I whirled away from it, faced the wide expanse of the bowl floor down on which I had looked from the brink of the sheer, mile-high cliff that closed it in. Directly ahead, across a perfectly level stretch of fused rock, was a low building, blue-gray and windowless like the one out of which I had just come, but tiny in comparison to it. To my right and quite a distance farther off, there was another, somewhat larger, and to one side of it one about a quarter its size.

If I recalled correctly the layout of Adalon seen from above, the nearer structure was . . .

"Mercury," Daster supplied. "Correct. And the farther one is Earth, with its Moon. Mars is hidden behind Sun. You are the first of our — guests — to perceive that Adalon is planned to portray the Solar System." He seemed approving, and I could not help being a little pleased with myself.

"You call the buildings after the planets they represent?" I noted.

"Yes," the Doctil agreed.

There were a few Plebos about, grotesque caricatures of humanity with their tremendous heads, their bulbous bodies, their writhing, tentacular arms. They were moving briskly across the terrain in various directions, but they weren't walking. They stood on little wheeled platforms of the same odd metal of which the stratcars were built, and these were rolling swiftly along the trackless pavement. I could see no steering wheels or other means of control; the peculiar vehicles stopped and started and changed direction almost as if they were endowed with some queer life of their own.

One, somewhat larger than the others, and unoccupied, came toward us. It was like a child's playcart, except that it had no sides, but at the front end there was a boxlike protuberance from which rods ran to either end of the forward axle. As it neared I heard a low burr of machinery. It came up to us, wheeled around and stopped.

"They're worked by remote radio control," I decided, remembering a demonstration I had seen in New York's Museum of Science and Industry. "But I can't see the advantage. It must require an operator for each one and . . ."

"The rider of each *rado* is its operator," Daster interrupted, motioning for me to get on to the thing and doing so himself. We faced forward on it and it started rolling smoothly towards Earth. "I summoned this one, for instance, and am directing it now." It deftly avoided collision with another, whose Plebo rider lifted his tentacles in salute to Daster.

"Where's your sending set?" I challenged skeptically. I was getting more used to the Doctil's weird appearance, more aware of him as an individual with whom I could talk naturally, whom I could question. "You haven't anything in your hands and certainly you can't be hiding it anywhere about you."

"My brain is the only sending set I need for the rado."

"Oh now, listen! You don't expect me to believe that, do you?"

"I do. You have information and intelligence enough to understand it. Even in your time it was already becoming known that the processes of the brain and nervous system are essentially electrical in character. My control of the rado through what you would call will alone is merely a projection of the same manifestation of energy by which you wiggle your great toe."

"I get it," I exclaimed. "Just as radio is a development of telegraphing over wires. Then . . . then your means of communication, my hearing you without your speaking aloud, must be something similar."

"Precisely. Except that in that case your brain is acting as a receiving unit. It has not yet evolved sufficiently for it to be used efficiently as a transmitter, although our researches seem to indicate that some among those of your time did have that power in a rudimentary manner."

"There have been some experiments with it," I recalled. "At Duke University, for instance. They call it telepathy, extra-sensory perception, and — " I broke off. We were being carried past the House of Mercury. Coming around from behind it and turning towards us was another rado like the one we rode. On this, beside a Plebo, was a man like myself.

Not quite like myself. He was much taller, built in a heavier mould. His colossal frame was clothed in a flowing dark robe down whose front flowed a luxuriant, silver-white beard. His massive features were swarthy, broadly sculptured, his nose wide-winged and bent-ridged, his brooding eyes sunken beneath shaggy white brows. I thought of Rodin's statue of Jehovah in the Metropolitan. There was about this man the same Semitic cast of countenance, the same consciousness of majesty, the same quiet strength.

His rado, shot by us and ran swiftly toward the great building we'd just quitted, too swiftly for me, startled as I was, to call to him. "Who is that?" I demanded, twisting to Daster. "Who is that man?"

"His name is Elijah," was what the Doctil responded. "He was known as a Prophet of Israel in the age to which he belongs."

"But . . ." I gasped. "But Elijah was taken up to Heaven in a chariot of fire."

"So it was reported by Elisha, his disciple, who saw him go. The sun struck through the whirlwind of desert dust that parted them and gave it the appearance of flame, and when it was gone, Elisha too was gone." And then, quite simply, quite convincingly, Daster the Doctil said, "I saw it. I was there."

Francois Villon! Elijah! A pattern, a faint and appalling pattern, was forming at the back of my brain. Elijah:

Prophet in Israel. *Francois Villon:* Thief, Lover and Poet. I had read those names not very long before. On a yellowed, crumbling page they had been, part of a list headed, The Vanished. And on the page before that one, in rubbed italics, had been words that now took on a heart-squeezing significance:

Like so many whispering whorls of dust they went out of space and out of time, to what Otherwhere no one still among us knows, and none will ever know.

"None will ever know." But I knew. Very terribly I knew where Elijah and Villon and I had come. And Evelyn Rand.

This, this Adalon, was that incredible Otherwhere out of space and out of time!

CHAPTER 11
THE SCENT OF DREAMS

THE RADO ROLLED up to the grayblue wall of the building called Earth, stopped. Daster dismounted and I followed, my mind occupied with trying really to comprehend the conclusion to which it had come.

There was an opening here like the exit from the gigantic central structure. The Doctil waited for me to enter this before him. Inside there was a tunneled passage similar to the one in the House of the Sun, lit similarly with a twilight glow. But the floor of this did not move. The corridor went in about five feet, turned sharply right. It did not rise as that other had but went straight on. I walked along it too shaken to be fully aware of what I was doing, too shaken to be curious about my surroundings or my destination.

Up to the moment when Daster had told me the long-bearded man in the dark mantle was Elijah, *and I had believed* him, I had neither accepted nor rejected the actuality of any of my strange experiences. Perhaps I can best explain what I mean by an analogy. Once, on Okinawa, a shell fragment slashed my leg. I sat on the ground staring at the inch-deep gash in my flesh, at the blood welling out of it and for minutes had absolutely no emotion about it at all. I knew it was my leg that was sliced to the bone. I knew it was my blood pouring out. I knew that it was beginning to hurt damnably but all of that seemed to concern me not at all. Then someone had yelled, "Hell. They got the lieutenant," and visions had smashed into my brain of that leg having been chewed up so badly that it would have to come off, of my going around on crutches all the rest of my life.

A medic had put a tourniquet on me in a hurry, that time, and penicillin and plasma and the miracle men they call Army surgeons had made my leg good as new more quickly than I'd had any right to expect. But this thing I was up against now was different. Nobody was going to get me out of this mess. Nobody could. It was strictly and entirely up to me, myself.

That was a laugh! These people in whose power I was, these Adalonians, had demonstrated themselves to be masters of forces I could not even begin to conceive. The Adalonians could read my thoughts at will, could sense them almost before I was aware of them myself. Against them I was far more at a disadvantage than the most benighted Australian aborigine had been against the invading white man equipped with all the knowledge and the tools of civilization. I was finished. Kaput. Done for. It was fantastic to imagine that I could do anything against them. Anything at all.

If I behaved myself, did exactly as they told me, maybe they'd let me live for a while. That was the best I could hope for.

"You have come to a wise decision," I heard behind me. "You are quite helpless, and your realization of that will save you a great deal of difficulty." I actually heard someone say that. It was no echo inside my brain, it was sound, a voice, in my ears! I twisted around.

It wasn't the Doctil I stared at, my jaw dropping. It was a man properly proportioned, properly clothed in a brown suit very much like my own. He was about my height too, but he was older than I. Gray-haired, high-foreheaded, blinkingly near-sighted, he had a distinctly professional air. He might just have stepped out of some university lecture hall.

"Who-?" I spluttered. "Who are you? Where did you come from?"

He smiled rather vaguely. "I am still Daster," he said in that thin, old man's voice. "I have merely assumed this appearance because I have found that my real form disturbs the natural reactions of the person we are about to join, and it is important that this should not happen. Now, if you'll step aside so that I can get to that door . . ."

There *was* a door, an honest-to-goodness wooden door with a knob of black glass, beside me where an instant before there had been only blank wall.

Daster stepped by me to the door. It is an index to my state of mind that I found more astonishing than his metamorphosis, more surprising than the sudden materilization of the door, the fact that he lifted his hand and knocked on it. The familiar, sharp rap of knuckles on wood was startling.

Someone inside said, "Come."

I knew that voice, though I'd never heard it before, and my breath caught in my throat. Daster's blue-veined hand was on the doorknob. He was turning it. It seemed to me I was watching a slow-motion film, of a knob turning, of a door swinging open. It swung outward toward me, so that it blocked my view of what was behind it. Daster went past its edge, was screened by it.

Very faint in my nostrils was the perfume of arbutus and crocuses and hyacinths, and the evasive scent of leafbuds, the fragrance of spring in a countryside I could never hope to see again. And underlying this was the redolence I could not name, the very breath of dreams.

"I have brought you someone," I heard Daster say, "whom I know you will be happy to see." I realized that I was going past the edge of that door, that I was going into the room on which it had opened.

She was standing with her white fingers to the soft round of her breast, her lips half-parted. There was an attitude of expectancy about the poise of her slim, young body, a look in her cool gray eyes that seemed to say she had been waiting for me all the time I had searched for her. She was not beautiful. Even in that moment I knew that in the ordinary sense of the word she was not beautiful, her features were too irregular for that, her mouth too generous. But her hair was a misty amber cloud, and the throbbing curve of her throat was a lilting line of melody. There was strength in her small blunt chin and in her face an aching sweetness.

"John March," Daster's voice said, somewhere to one side. "And —"

"Evelyn Rand," I put in, deep-throated.

A smile touched her lips, sunshine caressing rose petals. "You know me, Mr. March? I don't recall our having met."

"We haven't. I have never seen you. But I know you. I am one of your guardian's junior attorneys and I've been hunting for you for all of two weeks."

"Two weeks?" Her little frown of puzzlement was intriguing. "I don't understand. If Mr. Sturdevant wanted to get in touch with me why didn't he call me up? He knows my number and I was home till yesterday morning."

"You were . . ." I stopped myself. Something queer here. Something very queer. Daster was watching us. I didn't like the way he was watching us. His eyes were too glittering, too feverishly eager. "Of course you were," I said vaguely. "I . . . I confused you with another client.

"I shall leave you," the Adalonian interrupted. "I have some matters to attend to." He was moving toward the door. "I shall return in a little while." Turning to him, I became aware of the room, a quietly furnished living room; rugs, furniture, very like those I was accustomed to all my life. Except for one thing. There were two other doors, but there was no window. No sign of one.

The door closed on Daster, and I was alone with Evelyn Rand.

She'd come close. Her fingers were on the back of my hand, cold. "Tell me," she breathed. "What did you mean when you said you have been hunting for me for two weeks?" Her pupils were widening and the color was draining from her lips.

"I said that I was mistaken, didn't I?" It was clear that she was bewildered, and afraid. "Another client . . ."

"You said that, but it isn't true. A veil dropped over your eyes when you said it." Her hand had closed on mine now, was clinging to it. I wanted to take her in my arms. I wanted to hold her tightly, to still the flutter of her pulse in her neck, like the hurried beat of a frightened bird's heart. "Tell me what kind of place this is. Tell me who they are, in there." Her free hand jerked to one of the closed doors. "Tell me what's happened to me."

All the strength was running out of her, all the courage. She was on the verge of breaking. The Lord alone knew how long she'd been holding herself together by sheer will, how long she'd been facing down her fears. She'd been surrounded by a strangeness she could not understand and she'd held her terror of it tight within her. Now I'd come, someone she recognized to be her own kind, and abruptly the burden had become too great for her.

"Easy," I told her. "Take it easy." The truth would be better for her, kinder, than any lie that probably would be disproven at once. But what *was* the truth? "I don't know very much about it myself but I know there's nothing to be scared of. We're both in something of a mess, and we've got to be brave and sensible and figure out together just what it is and just how to get out of it."

The idea was to let her know that she had help, but also to make her feel that she had to take hold of herself and cooperate. It was like rescuing a drowning person. If you let them go hysterical on you they'll go down and drag you with them, but if you get across to them that they've got to do something for themselves you can get somewhere. It worked. She let go of my hand, straightened and smiled wanly. "I . . . I'm all right now." But there was still dread under the surface of her eyes. "You . . . are you a doctor?"

"A doctor? What makes you — " And then I got it. The poor kid! "Look here." I took hold of her shoulders. "Look into my eyes, and listen to me. I'm not a doctor and this is not a sanitarium and you're not crazy." I said that slowly, with all the conviction I could put into it. "You're as sane as algebra. Not only you, but the man who told you he is Francois Villon is sane, and the man who calls himself Elijah is sane. That is who they really are, unbelievable as it may seem."

I knew she'd spoken with Villon, and I guessed that she must have spoken with others out of time. It was quite natural for her to think them suffering from delusions. From what he had said she must have seen Daster in his real shape, and been convinced that she too was the victim of hallucinations. The only reasonable conclusion would be that this was a madhouse and she an inmate.

"You believe me," I went on. "You must believe me. Whatever else is wrong, you are not mad. Do you believe me?"

She nodded.

"Say it. Say it aloud. 'I know that I am sane. Whatever has happened, whatever is going to happen, I am sane.'"

"I know that I am sane." Her voice was just above a whisper, her lips tremulous. "Whatever has happened, whatever is going to happen, I am sane." But her eyes were more natural now, the fear was gone from them. "Thank you, John March. Oh, thank you."

"Nothing to thank me for yet. Wait till I've gotten us out of this." I made myself sound brisk, confident. I was very far from either. About two minutes ago I'd decided that I hadn't the slightest chance of extricating myself from the predicament in which I'd found myself, had resigned myself to take whatever the Adalonians wanted to hand me. Nothing had changed since then. "That sofa looks comfortable." Nothing except that now I had Evelyn Rand to look out for. "Let's sit down and talk things over."

I put my hands in my trouser pockets and strolled over to the couch I'd indicated, giving a good imitation of nonchalance. Some coins jingled in the right-hand pocket, in the left I felt a wallet and a latch-key in its little leather case. Evelyn Rand was coming along beside me, her pale blue dress whispering against the thighs of those long, free-swinging legs of hers.

We might have been any boy and gal about to spend a pleasant evening in a New York living room. Except that there was no window in this living room, and that not far beyond its walls a man named Francois Villon was suffering some unimaginable fate.

No. The Twentieth Century couple we most resembled was a Jewish one in some Berlin parlor, pretending that all was right with the world while all the time they were aware of horror outside, and the inevitable closing in of doom upon them. I knew this was only a brief respite, a short moment of truce our captors were according us for some inscrutable reason of their own.

I kept my face averted from Evelyn till I was certain I had gained control of it, till I was certain she could not read from it the dread and the despair that were in my thoughts. If I had known then what there was to dread, what there was to despair of, I should not have been able to conceal those emotions from her.

CHAPTER 12

"WALK INTO MY PARLOR"

"SUPPOSE WE BEGIN," I said, when Evelyn Rand and I were seated, "with your story. You started out to go to church. You went around the corner — and then?"

"And then I had a curious feeling that I was about to meet someone who'd been waiting for me a long time." Just the tip of a tiny ear showed from beneath the honeycolored cap of her hair. "The street was full of people with Sunday shining in their eyes, but it wasn't any of them. It was someone else. I'd had that same feeling, dreamlike but altogether actual, once before."

"In Faith Corbett's garden in Westchester," I murmured, "the day before you went away to college."

"Yes." She didn't seem at all surprised that I knew. "That time I was sure Johnny, the boy I'd pretended to play with all the lonely years till he'd become very real and very dear, was about to meet me at the gate — Oh!" She broke off. "Your name is John, isn't it? And you've got reddish brown hair and eyes too, like my Johnny, and a cleft in your chin."

"Wait," I cut in, a cold breath blowing on the base of my skull. "Wait. Let's not talk about me. Let's go back to Sunday."

"I was excited, though I kept telling myself I was being very silly." Her gaze stayed on my face, and her eyes were luminous. "Halfway down the block I stopped, because there was a strange little man in front of me, bowing to me with old fashioned courtesy.

"'You are Evelyn Rand,' he said, in a whispery sort of far-away voice. He'd popped up so suddenly, right there. He was so queer-looking too, bald, with a round face and tight, yellowish skin and a head a little too large for him."

"Achronos Astaris!" I exclaimed, under my breath.

"What? What did you say?"

"I've met your little man." And how! "But go on."

"I admitted my name. I was a bit nervous, but I wasn't afraid. Not yet. There was something about him I didn't like, but nothing could happen to me there in the heart of New York, with crowds all around. 'And you are . . . ?' I asked.

"'A friend of Faith Corbett's,' he told me. 'Your old nurse — I've come from her for you.'

"'Faith's ill,' I cried. 'She's dying!'

"The little man shook his bead. 'No. Not dying. But if you'll be good enough to come with me. It will not take long.' He put his hand on my elbow, as if to urge me, and a strange thing happened. The buildings, the street, everything, melted into grayness, everything but the little man's eyes. Those eyes got larger and larger. I seemed to plunge into them. The grayness seemed to be rushing by me at a perfectly awful speed, and it was empty, most dreadfully empty. And then — and then —"

She stopped, her pupils widening again, the faint rose that had spread under her skin when she'd spoken of my resemblance to her imaginary Johnny fading to a transparent pallor.

"Steady, Evelyn," I said softly. "Steady." My hand slid along till it reached hers. "Look. You don't have to go on. I can guess the rest."

"But I want to, John. I want to tell you."

I'm no Galahad. I'd held hands with girls before, and done plenty more than hold hands. But there was something about the feel of hers, something about the way her icy fingers took hold of mine, quite simply, quite naturally. "Go ahead." I couldn't trust myself to say any more, just then.

"The grayness got solid. I was standing among a lot of queer rocks. Beside me there was something out of a nightmare, a Thing with a tremendous head, and awful eyes, and —

"Skip the rest. I've seen them."

"You have! Then it was real!"

"It's real enough," I answered dryly. "Too real to suit me. What happened next?"

"I don't know. I must have fainted. The next thing I knew I was in this room, lying on this sofa, and the gentleman who brought you here was telling me that I was all right, that I must not be frightened. But I was. I was terrified, though I couldn't seem to do anything but lie here and stare at him. Mr. Daster kept on talking, low-voiced and very soothingly. I . . . it's funny, John . . . but I can't remember what he said. I can remember only that little by little my heart stopped pounding, and the iron band that seemed to be squeezing my brain was gone and I — I think I fell asleep."

They had been kinder to her than to me, I thought. Thank God for that.

"I woke up," Evelyn went on, "with the feeling that someone was in the room. Someone was, a girlish looking little boy about nine or ten years old, with the saddest eyes I've ever seen. He smiled shyly at me and spoke in beautiful French, apologizing for his intrusion. I asked him who he was, and, John, he said he was Citizen Louis Charles, *cidevant* Louis Bourbon, heir to the throne of France."

"The Lost Dauphin," I exclaimed. "It checks. By all that's holy, it checks. He was on the list too."

"What checks?" she demanded. "What list are you talking about?"

"Never mind. I'll tell you about it later." I had a pretty clear idea of what happened next, from what I'd seen and what I'd gathered from her manner. "When the boy said that, you were sure he was mad. Then you met the others he spoke of and each one told you he was someone else who couldn't possibly be alive, and you were sure that you'd lost your mind and were in an asylum with a lot of other lunatics." I wanted to get her past that part. "Isn't that so?"

"Yes," she breathed. "What else could I think?"

"Certainly not the truth, the utterly incredible truth." The jittery look was in her eyes again. I'd learn the rest of what I needed to know later. "Look here, young lady, you've been talking long enough, it's about time you gave another fellow a chance. One thing though. You haven't been harmed, have you, or annoyed in any way?"

"No. But the time has been so long, so awfully long. I never knew a day and a night and half of another day could seem like eternity."

A day and a night. I checked myself. It was two weeks since she'd vanished. "Is that how long it is since you came here?" Did time run differently here? If it did that was proof, indubitable proof, that this was not some hidden-away place on Earth, as I still half-hoped. "Are you sure?"

She shrugged. "I'm not sure of anything. But I've only slept once, in the bedroom in there," she nodded at the door opposite to that to which she had pointed before. "And I've only eaten four meals. Why do you ask?"

Here was something else that I'd have to break to her carefully. "Because that fits in, too, to my idea of what this is all about. Listen to me, Evelyn. We're involved in something very strange, something almost uncanny. It's quite unbelievable, but we've got to believe it, because it's true. And because the only way we can get out of the predicament we're in is to understand it thoroughly. What's more, we've got to keep remembering, always, that we can and will find a way out, no matter who or what opposes us, no matter how impossible it seems."

I was talking for my own benefit as well as hers. I needed the confidence I was preaching.

"I understand." Her grave, gray look was fixed on my face and I read utter trust there. "You'll find a way out, I know you will." I didn't deserve that. I was just a confused, bewildered guy up against something too big for him. And I was altogether a stranger to her.

Or was I? There was that imaginary playmate of hers, who had my name, my features. There was the way she had become a very real, very intimate person to me long before I'd seen her, a person so real that I loved her before I set eyes on her. "Now that we're together at last, Johnny," she said, "I'm not afraid any longer. I'm not afraid of anything at all."

I couldn't let her down after that. Now could I? "Thanks, Eve," was all that I said, but she got what I meant. "Now let me tell you my experience." I let her have it, lock, stock and barrel, the essentials of everything I'd been through from the time Astaris had shown up in the Art Gallery to when Daster had brought us together. Of *almost* everything. For no good reason I left out mention of the carved black stone I'd found in her nursery, the gem whose replica was so paradoxically painted into her portrait. Because it was so nerve-shaking I omitted the incident of the ambush on the entrance plain and the fate of the two who had attacked Kass. And I left out Villon's cryptic speculation about the implication of the arrangement of the buildings in Adalon for another very good reason, a reason that was sending ripples chasing up and down my spine at the same time as it tightened my throat with helpless anger.

We were being spied on

As we talked I had gradually become aware of this, I don't know how or why. We were alone in that room. The doors, keyholeless, were shut. There was no sign of a crack or peephole in the walls and nothing hung on them that might conceal one. I had heard nothing out of the way.

Perhaps I had become sensitized, vaguely, to the waves of nervous force of which Daster had spoken. Whatever it was, I was conscious, as distinctly as one is conscious of a stare on the back of one's neck, that our every word, our every thought, our every emotion, was being observed and noted.

CHAPTER 13

THE LOTTERY OF DOOM

THERE WAS NOTHING I could do about it. There was no point in alarming the girl by telling her about it, no point in undoing what I had accomplished in setting her at her ease. Moreover, there might be some advantage in concealing from the Adalonians my awareness of what they were up to. And so I went on as I had intended.

"It all adds up to something like this, Evelyn. In some quite incomprehensible way, we have been carried off to a region that isn't on Earth at all, that in all likelihood isn't anywhere in the Solar System. Tentatively, at least, we've got to assume that what's been hinted to me is true, that those who have done this, the people I've been calling the Adalonians for lack of a better name, come from Earth too, but from an Earth far, far older than that which we know. Whether this is so or not, they have a knowledge and powers far greater than we can conceive.

"One of these powers seems to be that of ranging backward and forward in time at will, for not only we, but other individuals from a number of far separated periods in Earth's history, have been gathered here by them. How they do this I can't even begin to think, but there is no question that they have done it, and done it with a definite purpose. That purpose seems to be the acquisition of some information from us, some knowledge that, omniscient as they seem, they lack."

"If you're right about them, what could we possibly know that they don't?"

I shook my head. "Don't ask me that. But you must remember that the knowledge of a race is not always cumulative. Mankind forgets, just as every man forgets. Haven't we often run across hints that the ancients had skills, arts, of which all trace has been lost? To take a simple thing, the secret of Michaelangelo's pigments has been lost."

"And no one knows how Stradivarius got that wonderful tone in his violins," Evelyn put in.

"Exactly. But I have a notion that what the Adalonians, want from us is something we don't know ourselves that we know." I was thinking of the questions that Astaris and Kass had put to me. "And even finding out what it is isn't quite as important as discovering why they need the information they're after, why they are so eager to get it. I don't think it's merely scientific curiosity, they're going to too much trouble for that."

The uneasy sense of being watched, listened to, persisted. It was a creepy feeling, that of an unseen Presence hovering over us, of privacy invaded and of being helpless to avoid it. A damned uncomfortable feeling.

"Why is it important, Johnny?" Evelyn asked. "How would it help us to know all this?"

Her inquiry seemed to crystallize something that all this time had been at the back of my mind. "Because, Eve, if we know what they want and why they want it, we may be able to trade it for our release. We can't fight them, but I have an idea that we can dicker with them."

I didn't say that for her. I said it for him, for whomever it was that was listening. And I waited for some indication that he had heard, for some sign that my offer was accepted. As if she sensed what I was about Evelyn waited too, her damask lips a little parted, her fingers tightening on my hand, tightening and trembling almost imperceptibly.

No hint came that I'd been heard, no slightest hint that what I'd said had made any impression on the eavesdropper. I was a fool to have hoped it. The Adalonians were too certain of their powers, too completely certain. They would squeeze us dry of what they wanted from us, and then toss us away like so much pulped orange. Toss us to the Drina.

"What is it, Johnny?" Evelyn exclaimed. "What's scared you?"

"Scared me?"

"Your face went white all of a sudden, your lips gray." Small wonder they had, with the vision flashing across my mind, of her graceful form swallowed within a gray-purple loathesome mass, of her lovely body blurring, melting away . . .

"White?" I laughed. "No wonder I'm white. I'm so hungry I'm carnivorous now, and in about a half an hour more I'll turn cannibalistic. If you don't look out I'm likely to be lunching on you."

Her laugh, responding to mine, was a silvery tinkle. "I'm afraid I wouldn't afford you much nourishment, I'm all skin and bones." She broke off. "Remember when I said that last, Johnny? We were playing we were shipwrecked and we were arguing which one of us should eat the other. Do you remember?"

The queer thing was that I seemed to. Very, very dimly, as if it were something I'd dreamed. But all kids play shipwreck sometime or other. "How did it come out?" I asked. "Who ate whom?"

"You ate me, of course. I meant you to, all the time."

"That must have been a pretty swell meal. But all kidding aside, is there any prospect of being fed around here?" Get a grip on yourself, chump, I was saying to myself. Keep your eye on the ball. "Or am I doomed to slow starvation?" Part of me was aching to take her in my arms, and never let her go. And another part of me was telling me that was just what I must not do. "A tenderloin about four inches thick, with the blood oozing out from under a blanket of mushrooms and onions, would just about put the roses you seem to miss so much back in my pallid cheeks." I sucked said cheeks in and pressed my hands to my middle, groaning.

This clowning brought that musical laugh from her again. Which was my intention. "It's quite likely your life may be saved," she said, "very shortly." She glanced at her wrist, at a tiny dial, no bigger than a fingernail, cased in crystal and clinging there by grace of a bracelet braided from platinum strands. "It's almost noon!" She rose from the couch, "Come on. We'll go see."

As I got to my feet, I was thinking: Almost noon! But it was almost noon when I started for Brooklyn, and that was hours ago. "Are you sure that's the right time, Eve?" I asked aloud. "Hasn't your watch stopped?"

"Of course not. I wound it this morning and it was going then." She was walking toward one of the doors and I was following her.

"How many times have you wound it since you left for church," I asked softly.

"Only that once, Johnny. Why?"

"Oh nothing. I thought anything as small as that would have to be wound every couple of hours or so." Nothing?

It was the indisputable proof that we were somewhere else than on Earth. Evelyn might have been deceived as to elapsed time, that faint of hers might have been a coma lasting for days, but the little mechanism on her wrist could not be deceived. Measured by Earth time she had started for church more than two weeks ago, but she'd only had to wind her watch once since then, and it had not stopped. Time ran differently here, there could be no question of that, and the rest followed inevitably.

Evelyn opened the door and a strange polyglot of voices came through to me. The room we entered was large, high-ceilinged. It was as windowless as the one from which we came. But that one had been empty save for the two of us. A dozen or so men were in here.

And such men! The one I first set my eyes on was olive-skinned, his face angular. He wore a short-skirted robe diagonally striped in vivid coloring, and leather sandals whose thongs were crisscrossed about his muscular legs. His mop of black, kinky hair came down on either side of his head almost to the jaws and it was square cut. He might have stepped down from a mural in the Egyptian Room of the Museum.

He was conversing, more by signs than words, with a blonde giant dressed in skins, his yellow shock bristling with strange ornaments of bone. A Briton barbarian from long before the invasion of the Picts or I missed my guess. Beyond them was a group whose members were a togaed Roman, an American Indian in full panoply of quill-embellished buckskin and a fierce eyed Mongolian jingling with hammered silver accoutrements who might well have been a lieutenant of Genghis Khan.

To describe all the occupants of that long chamber would be to make a catalogue of all the races of Man through five thousand years of history. It would require an etymologist to name all the languages they spoke. In speech, in customs, in origin, they were utterly different. But there was one thing they had in common, one thing I felt at once, in the moment I entered among them.

That thing was betrayed by a tautness of the cords in their necks, by a continual shifting of their eyes to the door that from its location I knew opened on the corridor that had brought me to Evelyn, by a jerkiness of movement that could come only from almost unendurable tension.

One of the grizzled elevator men in the building that houses the offices of Sturdevant, Hamlin, Mosby and Garfield was a Russian aristocrat, an ex-Baron. He'd been captured by the Bolsheviks during the Revolution, had been imprisoned for some years, had escaped by some fluke or other. We'd gotten friendly, and once he'd told me of the jails of the Cheka, of the rooms in which the prisoners were gathered, each one knowing that sooner or later he would be called out to be executed, none knowing when, or if he would be the next, or if he would be the last. All knowing that doom was certain, and waiting, waiting, waiting . . .

They were like that, exactly like that, the men assembled here, except that their case was worse because they did not know to what fate they were to be summoned. They knew only that it would be something less merciful than death.

"There's someone here I want you to meet, Johnny," Evelyn said. Her hand on my arm, she guided me to a corner where stood two men and a boy, a little withdrawn from the others, a little aloof.

The boy was the one she had already described to me; the Lost Dauphin, son of Marie Antoinette and the ill-fated Louis XVI of France. His clothing was almost in rags, his toes thrust through the broken uppers of his shoes and there was a bruise on the side of his face. The mark of some brutal jailer's blow, I thought, recalling that History's last certain glimpse of him was in a prison of the Terror.

One of the men with the Dauphin was a tall and stately Teuton, square-jawed, black polled. There was something of the military in his posture, but the long-fingered hand with which he seemed to be fumbling for a sword hilt was the sensitive hand of a musician, and his haggard countenance was too eloquent of thought to be a soldier's. I was afterward to learn that this was John Orth, Archduke of Tuscany, son of Princess Marguerite of the Two Sicilies and closest friend of that scion of the Emperor Franz Josef of Austria who died for love at Mayerling.

It was the last of that trio who interested me most.

He was shorter than his companion, broader of shoulder and chest. His powerful body was swathed in a cloak of dark purple, and if the little Dauphin's pose was kingly, this man's was imperial. His hair, his beard, were blonde and silken, the eyes that watched me as we approached were the deepest blue I'd ever seen and keen as the thrust of a rapier. At one instant there was a sad sweetness about his mouth, almost effeminate, at the next it firmed and I knew that here was a man to venerate, and to fear.

He spoke as we came up to the group. "Ali, Maid Evelyn. Thou hast deprived us of thy sweet company too long." His voice, though low, was sonorous and it was mellow, and something inside of me thrilled to it. "And who is this thou bringest with thee?"

"Someone from my own time and age. John March."

I'll be damned if I didn't have the impulse to go down on one knee when he turned to look at me. "Johnny," Evelyn said, "This is King Arthur of Britain."

"John March," he repeated, and lifted his hand. I didn't know whether to shake or kiss it, that's how bewildered I was. I did neither.

I did neither because in the next instant Arthur was no longer paying any attention to me, nor I to him. Because there was another voice in that room, a rasping, imperative voice. The voice that all its occupants were waiting for, saying a name. Saying two names.

"John March. Evelyn Rand. You are wanted."

The lottery of doom had been drawn again, and it was our names that had been drawn!

CHAPTER 14

A DEAL WITH DISASTER

EVELYN STIFFENED, BESIDE me, her winsome face drained of all color. "Us," she whispered. "Johnny. They have come for us."

Across the high-ceilinged chamber the strip of secret blackness between the portal's edge and its jamb widened with a fearful slowness . . .

"Chin up, Eve." My arm went around the girl's slender waist and I pulled her quivering body against my side. "Head up." My voice was steady, though how I contrived to keep it so I still do not comprehend. "There's nothing to be afraid of. Nothing at all." My forehead was wet with a chill sweat.

The togaed Roman backed away from the widening door, his haughty, patrician features gray with terror. A mustached Tartar lurched against a wing-helmeted Viking from the Fjords.

"Don't let them take me," Eve moaned. "Don't let them —"

"And that we shall not, Maid Evelyn," King Arthur's deep-chested tones cut across her plea. "As long as there remains breath in our body and strength in our arms." He shoved past me to interpose himself between us and the grotesque beings who now were entering the now open doorway.

"Nor so long as I have powder and ball with which to defend you," John Orth added and ranged himself beside Arthur, his hand fumbling out from within his oddly cut jacket a long-barreled pistol whose butt was of silver intricately engraved. "Never has it been said that an Archduke of Tuscany failed to champion the cause of a maid in distress."

"Nor a Bourbon." The little Dauphin joined the three, somehow no longer a child as he whisked a stiletto from somewhere among his rags.

And toward those three from the past there advanced across the wide space that had cleared between them and the entrance three men of the dim future, two Plebos and Daster in his true shape. Arthur's purple cloak fell back from his arm and a sword flashed out, a great gleaming sword full four feet in length, its blade a shaft of silver light, its hilt jewelled gold. "Excalibur has not forgot its skill," he boomed, "nor its master his chivalry."

Written down all this seems mere rhodomontade, then it was rather splendid. The bald and bulbous skulls of the trio they defied held all knowledge — unimaginably transcending the magic of

Merlin, the esoteric powers to which Cagliostro laid claim. The ogling eyes could read our every thought, our every intention, almost before we were ourselves aware of them. The boneless, writhing tentacles could paralyze a man with agony, yet knowing all this Arthur, and Orth dared to challenge them with a sword, an ancient pistol and a stiletto.

A curious exaltation pounded in my veins as I stepped forward beside them, my empty fists clenched. And the Future Men advanced toward us, slowly, inexorably.

"Stop!" Orth cried. "Stop where you are or I fire." His pistol pointed at Daster. "Stop, I say."

The Adalonians kept advancing.

Orth's shot slapped my ears and orange-red flame lanced true to the Doctil's head. Utterly unperturbed, Daster came on, neither slackening nor hastening his relentless pace. "Missed," the Austrian groaned.

"The hell you did!" I jabbed a forefinger at a silvery splash on the wall directly behind the leader of the Future Men. "Your bullet went right through him." An eerie prickle scampered my spine. Though reason told me that this was only one more manifestation of that same mastery over the vibrations of matter that had enabled me to pass through a solid wall, no such scientific rationalization could make the occurrence less uncanny. "Bullets or steel are no good against them."

Now the Adalonians were within five feet of us and as though I'd not spoken Arthur's shaft rose, gleaming. "Halt," he roared, "an ye do not wish to feel the bite of a blade that hath never known defeat."

It was magnificent; and it was as pathetically ludicrous as Don Quixote's tilt with a windmill, as Canute bidding the tide retreat. It was worse than ridiculous, it was killing what faint hope I had of saving Evelyn from — "Daster!" Abruptly I was quite calm, my mind crystal clear. "Listen to me."

The Doctil's ear membranes pulsed and the three paused. I sensed Daster's question. "What is it, John March, that you wish to say?"

I pulled in a wheezing breath. Arthur and Orth were warriors and their weapons were futile against these strange beings who were our captors. I was a lawyer. My weapons were those of the weak against the strong; temporizing, compromise, stratagem.

"These men will fight you till you destroy them. You don't want to do that. You want them alive or you would not have brought them here in the first place."

"Exactly," the Doctil responded. "But they are of no use to us as they are. They must be taught to submit to our will."

"Taught? How? Read them, Daster, as I know you can. Read them and ask yourself if there is anything you can do, with all your powers, that will break their indomitable spirit."

His tremendous eyes moved to Arthur and Orth, and to the frail, boyish Dauphin. For what seemed an endless time the room was breathless.

Then: "No," the Adalonian sighed. "Even if we reduce them to their ultimate atoms they still will defy us." His thought flicked to the Plebos. He was giving them an order, "Feed them to the *drina* —"

"Wait!" I cut in. "Wait, Daster. I can tell you how you may bend them to your purpose. Will you listen to me?"

"Hold!" he told the Plebos. Then to me, "What do you propose?"

"What you cannot accomplish by force, you may by reason. Be frank with us. Tell us what you want of us and why, then offer us in exchange our release, our return to our own place and time, unharmed, and we will do our best to give you what you want. You have nothing to lose. You have to gain that for which you have gone to the trouble of gathering us here."

I sensed interest in the Doctil, then indecision. "If the rest of the Kintat agree —" He sank into the same sort of listening trance that had enveloped Kass on the brink of the plateau overhanging Adalon and I knew that he was in communication with his fellow Doctils, was transmitting my proposition to them.

"By the Holy Rood!" King Arthur growled, his countenance darkening. "We mislike this traffic with sorcerers. Merlin hath placed an enchantment upon Excalibur that rendereth it puissant against all evil witcheries, and we fainer would —"

"You damn fool," I blurted. "They could wipe you out in the twinkling of an eye, and you want to fight them. You're a blathering infant —"

"Silence, knave!" he thundered. "Thou art insolent." His eyes flashed blue lightnings and his sword rose in a swift, shining arc. "For less have we slain an hundred caitiffs." The blade swept down, straight for my skull swerved in the last instant to avoid Evelyn, who had leaped in front of me, her arms outspread.

"Arthur Pendragon!" she cried, stamping her foot. "Aren't you ashamed of yourself? Johnny's just saved your life and you try to kill him. You — you ungrateful —"

He glared at her, his great brows beetling. "This," he growled, "is not to be borne. We —" Abruptly his face was lit by a twinkling smile. "Nay. We cannot be wroth with thee, fair maid, who hath made endurable these dreary hours of our imprisonment. For thy sake we shall be merciful. Let this bold varlet crave our pardon on bended knee and it will be accorded."

"I'll be blasted if I will," I burst out, hotly. "I'm free, white and Amer —"

A soft palm across my lips cut me off. "Johnny," Eve whispered, her eyes pleading. "Do what he wants. Can't you see he's nothing but a big baby and has to be humored."

There was, indeed, something of the overgrown kid dressed up for 'let's pretend' about his purple trappings, something endearingly childish about the petulant scowl that had replaced his brief smile.

"Please," Eve begged. "Please, Johnny dear." Her hands tugged at my lapels and her mouth was moist and seductive. "For me."

"Oh well," I shrugged, and dropped to one knee. "I'm sorry I called you a fool, King Arthur," I muttered as graciously as I could manage.

"We grant thee our forgiveness." He held the back of his free hand to my lips. I might as well, I decided, make a complete ass of myself, so I kissed it and was rewarded by a grin from the hulking king and the tingling touch of Evelyn's fingertips on my cheek. "All the same," I grunted, scrambling to my feet, "you better cut out any idea of scrapping with these people if you ever want to see Camelot again."

"Camelot," Arthur sighed. "We misdoubt that we desire very greatly to return there. All our brave company that used aforetime to gather about the Table Round is scattered and the gray winds howl over our desolate land. The banners of our *gentil* and *parfait* knights are mired by fraternal strife, their shields besmirched with the breaking of their vows of fealty and fast friendship. All have abandoned us, all the noble chivalry who served God and us. Only Bedivere is left us, Sir Bedivere the Faithful."

That massively moulded countenance of his darkened and his lips twitched with pain. "But yestere'en, sore wounded in the Last Great Battle in the West, we gave Bedivere our blade Excalibur to cast back into the lake whence it came, and —" he broke off, staring at the storied sword he had named. "But we still have it! Now how-?"

"The legends say that a hand appeared out of the Lake and caught Excalibur from Bedivere, King Arthur." A thrill ran through me as I recalled the ancient tale. "And the legends say also that you did not die, which is the truth as we can see. But the story of your passing that has come down to us tells that three Queens bore you away from that misted battlefield on a black-swathed barge, and that I know to be false. Wasn't it in a whorl of dust that you vanished?"

"A whispering whorl of dust!" His deep blue eyes fastened on my face, and in them was a starry wonder, and a growing awe. "Aye. Out of the drab fog it came, out of the dun veil that shrouded the moans of the wounded, the throat-rattles of the dying. Out of the battle in which none were victorious it stole, and made us part of it. Now indeed this is such a matter of clairvoyance as is worthy of Merlin himself. How know you this, John March?"

"I know it, and I know many things that are beyond your understanding, Arthur Pendragon," I pressed my sudden advantage. "Which ought to convince you that you'd better take my advice, as you used to take Merlin's. You may be a grand fighter, but when it comes to using your brain —"

"Johnny!" Eve broke in. "Daster's coming out of his trance."

The Doctil's great orbs were focussed on me again. He was about to give me the Kintat's answer to my proposition and I seemed to empty out, inside; was a cold, shivering shell.

"You will come with me," I heard. "John March and Evelyn Rand." My heart sank. "And you also, Louis Capet, John Orth, and Arthur Pendragon."

I had won!

It was not to be long before I learned how hollow a triumph it was.

CHAPTER 15

THEY TOO CAN FEAR

EVELYN STAYED CLOSE to me as, led by Daster and shepherded by the two Plebos, we emerged from the strange, windowless House of Earth. A tightening of her fingers on my hand, a sharp inhalation, reminded me that this was her first sight of Adalon.

"The city's built on a rather interesting plan," I remarked, in an easy, conversational tone, "if you notice." I wanted to get her thoughts off what lay ahead of us. She was trying hard to be brave, but her face was dreadfully white and her little chin was quivering. "Look at that enormous building in the center, these eight others scattered around." For some reason Daster was not using rados for us. We were walking across the plaza towards the domed, enormous House of Sun.

"Scattered is right, Johnny." Eve smiled wanly. "I can't see what you mean by a plan."

"You can't? Look . . ." I pointed out how the pattern of the city was that of the Solar System. The others listened as attentively as Eve, though to Arthur what I was saying must have seemed the sheerest doubletalk. "I don't even think that it is by coincidence that our prison is the building corresponding to Earth. I think —"

"Pardonnez, Monsieur Marsh," the Dauphin interrupted. *"Ditez moi, s'il vous plait, qu'est ce que c'est qui mont, la bas?"* The thin-bodied lad's face was alive with a boyish, eager interest as he asked me what it was that lifted from the ground beyond the House of Mercury.

It was a lacy erection of crisscrossed, metallic beams, a spindling tower some five hundred feet high. "Jove!" I exclaimed. "They work fast, these Adalonians. There wasn't a sign of that when I passed here before, and that can't be more than an hour ago."

"It is not yet completed," Orth put in, in his too precisely enunciated English. "See there, Herr March, what goes on."

I discerned what he referred to. At the top of the tower, and at its base, what I had taken at first glance to be excrescences from its netted surface were machines, their gears turning, their piston arms shuttling frenetically.

I saw now that from the distant House of Pluto, clear across the plaza, a conveyor belt brought a stream of silvery girders to the machine on the ground. It seized them, swallowed them, disgorged them to another endless belt, changed in shape and studded with what from here looked very much like rivets.

Now the girders were carried almost vertically up to the machine at the tower's summit and the tower visibly grew upward as the machine moved upward with it, building it.

"Where are the workmen?" Eve demanded. "Those machines can't be simply working all by themselves."

"Oh," I replied airily. "An Adalonian somewhere out of sight is directing them by remote control."

"No," Daster corrected me. "They were set for their task by a stencilled pattern inserted into them. They will need no further supervision until the tower is finished."

"Of course," I made a quick recovery. "Just like our own jacquard looms for weaving intricately designed rugs and laces —"

That was lost on Louis. "How high will it be?" he asked the Doctil in that beautiful French of his. "When it is finished?"

"Its apex will be level with the lip of the encircling precipice."

"Whew!" I whistled. "That's a mile — five times the height of the Empire State —"

"What is its purpose," Orth inquired. "And why is it being built in such haste?"

Daster didn't answer him, not intelligibly, but the Austrian paled, his black eyes flashing, his hand straying to the sword-hilt that was not at his waist. "Easy, mister," I said softly, realizing that he had been rebuffed in no uncertain manner and in his resentment was on the point of an overt act that might undo all I had accomplished. "Easy. They've got a right to their secrets."

Nevertheless, the incident held a meaning I would have given a lot to fathom.

I glanced around the expanse we were crossing, wondering if there were any other significant changes I had failed to notice. It seemed to me that there were fewer Plebos than before. Those I did see, darting about on their rados, paid not the slightest attention to us but none failed to manifest a keen interest in the swiftly mounting tower. I had the impression that this interest was underlaid by some pressing anxiety.

Eve got it too. "There's worry in the air here," she whispered. "Fear almost. That thing's being built to protect them against something, and they won't feel safe until it's finished." As if to confirm her one of the Plebos accompanying us glanced upward. I caught the beginning of a quick thought-flash between him and Daster, curtained from me at once.

Up there at the brink of the cliff, a gray-purple shadow was flattened against the shimmering Veil of Ishlak. I saw it only momentarily, and then it had oozed away in a fashion that told me it was a *drina.*

Had it been spying on us? I wasn't sure whether that was my own speculation or whether I was intercepting some communication among the Future Men, but somehow I fancied a vast horde of the formless creatures bursting through the Veil, flowing down the immense, rocky ramparts, filling the bowl and swallowing every living being within it. So vivid was the illusion that my nerves drew taut.

"By our halidom!" King Arthur exclaimed. "So bright a bird we have never seen!"

It wasn't a bird that leaped from the Sun Dome. It was a stratcar that zoomed with blurring speed straight for the spot where the drina had peered down at us, hovered there for a split second and dived through the Veil. Once more, in that swift leap, I sensed alarm. The feeling of apprehension in the air of Adalon seemed to deepen.

Villon's voice came back to me, musing when Kass was ordered back to the wild and rocky tableland out of which he'd just conducted us, "Something is not as it should be among them. Dare we hope . . . ?"

I must blot that line of thought before Daster tuned in on it. Poor Francois! He was himself undoubtedly beyond hope by this time. His audacity, that a dozen times had saved him from hanging, would be futile against the Future Men. His luck had run out. Decidedly it had run out when Gohret took him —

"Look out, Johnny!" Eve's tug pulled me to a stop. "You almost walked into the wall."

Daster and the Plebos shooed us now into the corridor in the House of Sun out of which I had emerged not so long ago. Or was it the same? The passage we entered went straight into the depths of the structure. Nowhere was there any sign of the spiral ramp by which I had descended from the stratcar hangar. The doorway through which we had entered was the same. It must be the same; there had been only that single opening on this side of the great building . . .

But here, within, was a hall different in direction, in contour. A little while ago, in the House of Earth, a door had appeared in a blank wall beside me where an instant before there had been no door. In that same instant the great-headed, tentacular Daster had become a near-sighted, professorial human . . .

This impermanency of things apparently substantial was the most disquieting of all the phenomena of Adalon. Villon first, then Arthur and Orth and the Dauphin, had proved so altogether human that I had grown to accept, not through logic alone but with an inner conviction, the fact that our company had been assembled out of fifteen disparate centuries. Once oriented to such a telescoping of Time,

I could also comprehend that Daster and the other Adalonians were beings out of a remote Future.

But that flesh and bone, that solid stone, should be subject to unpredictable flux in shape and appearance still seemed incomprehensible.

It was, I had come to realize, this very flavor of unreality, menacing though it might be, that had enabled me to carry on. One may know utter, stifling terror in a nightmare, but in a nightmare one never quite despairs. One keeps on fleeing the inescapable succubus, one keeps on battling the unconquerable apparitions, because in the depths of one's being one somehow is still aware that awakening will come in the end.

I knew that this was no dream. I knew that the ghastly dilemma with which I was confronted would not be solved by a merciful awakening. And yet, because so much that had happened had the quality of a nightmare, I did not quite despair.

"Mordieu!" King Arthur exclaimed abruptly, halting. Eve's fingers dug painfully into my arm. I saw little Louis' narrow face go white. Orth's jaw ridged and my own throat was dry.

We were, with no gradation, with no warning of any kind, far within a chamber so vast that it dwarfed us to inconsiderable midges. Its walls were so immensely distant that they were misty limits to our sight, its ceiling so far above that it was a cloudy, indefinable dome. Only the floor beneath was definite, and this was a level expanse black as space itself. A gleaming, polished black it was, so that it seemed to have no substance and we appeared to be suspended in a featureless void, balanced sole to sole on our own inverted images.

In this gargantuan cavern there were only the five of us. Daster and the Plebos had vanished!

As a vaulted Gothic Cathedral is imbued with the very essence of the God to whose worship it has been erected, so was this unimaginable nave with some awesome Presence. It laid upon us, upon our hushed and crouching souls, a dark shadow of awed anticipation that had some fraternity with fear but transcended fear. It silenced us. It held us motionless. It held us peering wordlessly into the endless, empty reaches —

Far off there was movement. *Something* was coming toward us!

CHAPTER 16

"WHAT DO YOU WANT OF US?"

IT SEEMED AT FIRST a speck moving jerkily across that gleaming black expanse. There was no point of reference against which to measure the speed of its approach but it did approach, because very gradually it grew larger.

I heard King Arthur's sword slide from its scabbard. I heard the click of John Orth's pistol as he cocked it. I didn't bother to remind them how futile their weapons were. My own muscles were tautening across the back of my shoulders and in my thighs. For seconds I held my breath. Evelyn's hushed voice was in my ears. "They're men, Johnny. They're two men like us, not like the Adalonians."

Her eyesight must have been far keener than mine, because it wasn't till several heartbeats after that, that I made out the tiny forms. There was infinite weariness about the way they approached, a desperate fatigue that carried somehow across the distance between us. Once one of them fell, and it took a long time for the other to lift him to his feet.

And then, quite suddenly, they were near enough for us to see who they were.

"Villon!" the Dauphin exclaimed. *"Et le Prophete Elijah!"* He broke away from us, was scampering toward them, excited and eager as a ten-year-old boy might be expected to be and as reckless in his excitement of any precaution.

In the next instant the rest of us were streaming after him, our feet curiously making no sound on that marble-hard floor.

With a strange swiftness we had reached the two, were crowding around them. I had eyes for Villon alone. He held himself erect, but I could see that it was with tremendous effort that he did so. He was clothed as he had been when I had last seen him, and there was no wound visible about him, but all his jauntiness was gone and he was drained, somehow, of his infrangible spirit, emptied of all his indomitable courage.

"Francois!" I groaned. "What have they done to you? What have they done to you, man?"

He looked at me out of eyes that were like soot marks thumbed into hollow sockets. A shadow of his old mocking smile crossed his scarred lips.

"What have they done to me, my old?" A long shudder ran through him. "I know not. I know only that though they laid not a hand on me they have torn from my breast matters I kept secret from God Himself. I know only that I have babbled to them every thought I have had since I lay in the warm womb of my mother, though not a single word crossed my lips. I know only that they did not learn what they wished, and that I was about to be cast to the drina when some message came to them and I found myself here instead, this venerable Jew leading me across midnight's floor."

"But you must have seen something, heard something."

"Light only, John March. A blaze of white light about me and within me, and eyes in the light, the terrible eyes of our captors. Light that possessed me utterly. Eyes that read my very soul. And I read theirs too and —" He pulled the back of his hand across his seamed brow. In his eyes there was such horror as I hope never to see again in the eyes of any man.

"And what, Francois?" It was inflicting torture on him to ask, but I had to know.

He stared at me. "What?" His long-fingered hands went out from his sides, palms toward me, in a baffled gesture. "Why — I have forgotten, John." Dismay in his sultry look. "I remember that it was very terrible, but what it was, I have forgotten."

"Don't lie to me, Francois," I choked through the tightness in my throat. "The lives of all of us depend on what you've learned."

"More, far more than the lives of us seven is in balance," the poet answered, his countenance that of one who has died and been reborn with the memory of Hell searing him. "That much I know and the knowledge is a cloud of terror that invests me. But I swear to you, by the Crown of Thorns that was pressed on His brow, more I cannot remember and meseems that is because it is too terrible to recall."

"May Jehovah scourge them with the whips of His lightnings." The interruption was in sonorous Hebrew. "May He crush them with the bolts of His thunders." I understood it though I had not til that moment ever heard the ancient tongue spoken. "May He smite the sight from their eyes and the light of reason from their brains. May the plagues He sent upon the Egyptians rot them and their sons and their sons' sons unto the twentieth generation."

Intoning this curse, Elijah stood straight and tall and vibrant with an awful majesty. His gnarled hands were lifted high above the silver mane of his unkempt hair; his silver browed eyes were pits filled with a black and blazing fire and the nostrils of his craggy nose were pinched and quivering.

"May oblivion swallow them," he thundered, "and their names be a stink and an abomination even unto the end of Eternity. Hear me, Adonai, my God —"

"Your God," Francois broke in, "old man, your God, Who is ours also, has forsaken us. Here are only we seven and none else, and if we are to be saved it is we alone who can save ourselves."

Did I say that his courage had been drained out of him? I was mistaken.

"But how?" Evelyn's voice was thin with the new terror that their appearance had brought to her, to all of us. "How can we save ourselves, Francois?" Her hands were thrown out to him, appealingly, and they were trembling.

Villon turned lithely to her. He swept to his breast his wide-brimmed, cone-crowned hat, its bedraggled feather fluttering. "Nay, Evelyn of the honeyed hair, I must indeed be bemused that I have not yet observed your presence. I know now that we have naught to fear, for not even Lucifer could be so evil as to harm one so fair."

I didn't like that. I didn't like the bold admiration that had come into his look in spite of what he'd just passed through, in spite of the threat hovering over us. I didn't like, as far as that went, the way Eve had turned to him for help, nor the tender smile that brushed her white lips.

"Please," she murmured. "Please, Francois, answer me. How are we to save ourselves?"

He shrugged bony shoulders. "That, sweet maiden, is not for me. You have at your service a prophet of Israel, a king and a princeling, a duke and a barrister at the law. Apt these are in the art of arms and in the more subtle skills of tongue and brain, and surely so brave a company can devise ways to defeat our enemies. To myself, rhymster that I am, is left the more difficult task of essaying to enshrine your beauty and glamour in a ballade of gray eyes. Hmmmm." He laid a finger against the side of his rascally nose. "Let me see. Let me see . . ." He winked at me with the eye that was thus hidden from Evelyn!

That wink said, as clearly as though he had spoken, "Don't worry, my friend. I'm putting on this act just to calm her down. She's going to pieces and the only thing that will hold her together is a bit of skilled love-making."

"You might leave that to me," I thought, but I grinned at the Gallic effrontery, my heart warming again to the fellow. And then the grin was wiped from my face and my eyes were widening. The wall from whose direction Francois and I had come had swirled forwardl til it loomed starkly over us, black and shining as the floor, but, because it rose to unguessable heights, indescribably menacing. High up, a long, arc-roofed niche opened in it, a niche filled with a golden, luminous vapor.

For an instant of awestruck silence this aureate cloud billowed in upon itself, vibrant somehow and somehow alive. Somehow the very essence of life. Then, as we stared at it gaping-mouthed, it seemed to become more solid, to coalesce and divide and take on definition. Abruptly there was no longer a mist in that recess, but in a golden light that etched it sharply against its Styglan background, five figures gazed down at us.

Whether by some trick of perspective or in actuality, they seemed gigantic apparitions high in some ebony sky, godlike rather than mortal. But they had the bulbous bodies, the tentacles, the enormous heads, enormous-eyed, of the Future Men.

I recognized Daster at one end of their rank and Gohret at the other and so I knew the five to be the Kintat of Adalon. Some ineluctable, psychic effluvium emanated from them, invisible yet all but palpable, and there was nothing grotesque about those misshapen bodies, those tremendous occiputs.

It was we who were grotesque; we with our tiny brain pans, our clumsy hands, our groping, purblind eyes, dependent on inept physical senses for our small acquaintance with the world about us. We were only by courtesy human. They were truly human, and more than human. They had progressed immeasurably farther beyond us than we had beyond our furred and hand-footed simian ancestors who not so long ago roamed chattering in the jungle treetops. Our only right to existence was that we might be of service to them, and to be of service to them was high privilege.

I might actually have gone to my knees in genuflection had not Evelyn's cold fingers, just then, crept into the palm of my hand.

One does not easily strip oneself of pride in the presence of one's beloved. That silent appeal of Eve's restored my manhood. I straightened, the awed humility that had invested me sloughing off. Gohret's head-membranes pulsed once, at that, and I knew that by grace of that which lay between Evelyn Rand and myself I had won the first skirmish of a duel just beginning.

They were my opponents, that they were my masters was yet to be proved. As though we were about to appear against one another in the forum of some court, I weighed their qualities. Gohret was ruthless, coldly cruel, implacable. Daster, at the other extremity of the line, had a modicum of kindliness, a trace of benevolence that had impelled him to assume a shape that would not frighten Evelyn, and to answer my wanderings about the miracles of Adalon.

The Doctil next to Daster — Oddly, there was something familiar about him. Not in appearance, though there were the indefinable differences about him that made the Adalonians individuals. It was rather a matter of imponderables — I knew who he was. Astaris! The 'little man' who had appeared to me in the Madison Avenue Art Gallery that was worlds, and eons, distant from here. The emissary who had plucked me, and Evelyn, out of our own time and space.

He was the only one of the Five whose brooding gaze was other than general and unfocussed. He had singled out Eve for his attention, and there was a peculiar quiver about his tiny mouth —

"John March!"

The same demanding summons that had sounded in the House of Earth; it was the voice, not of any one of the Kintat, but of all five. It pulled me out in front of our little group. Eve clung to my hand and came with me, but I was scarcely aware of it.

"Yes?" My own voice was a hoarse croak.

"You have offered to yield to us that which we require of you, in return for your safe release. You have prevailed upon Arthur Pendragon, John Orth, Louis Capet and Evelyn Rand to accede to the treaty. We require that Elijah of Israel and Francois Villon signify their assent to it before we procede."

"Now indeed they are most gracious," I heard Villon mutter, behind me. "Can it be that they have found prophet and poet more obdurate than they deemed possible?"

I was reminded of the horror in his eyes, the horror of something he had learned but could not recall. Were the Adalonians tricking us into some promise we might have reason to regret?

"One moment, Doctils," I objected. "My words, as I remember, were 'Tell us what you want of us, and why. Offer us then our return to our own place and time, unharmed, and we will do our best to give you what you want.' That was my proposition, that was the proposition to which my friends agreed, and it is the one on which we stand."

"A Daniel," Elijah's murmur approved. "A very Daniel." But it was not so much this as another pulse at the sides of Gohret's head, a throb of his membrane that once more seemed to betray disappointment, that made me glad I'd said it. I was certain now that we had something with which to trade, something that they had gone to great lengths in their effort to obtain, and would go to greater. I would insist on knowing what it was before I would commit my clients to any irretrievable contract.

"We must know," I repeated, my tone firmer with the greater assurance this intuition gave me, "what you want of us, and why."

"What we want of you?" It was like a vast sigh filling all that enormous vault. Then there were no more words in my brain, but only an indescribable something beating upon it, swamping it —

Who was I to demand anything of those beings so superior to me? They were all wise, all-powerful. I was presumptous. I must withdraw — Fingers were tightening on my hand. Eve's fingers. Against my shoulder, on the other side, was the pressure of a comradely shoulder — Villon's. Behind me there was a rustle of moving feet, Arthur, Elijah, Orth and the Dauphin were crowding close.

"Precisely," a voice that was mine, yet somehow unwilled by me, sounded in my ears. It was not only my voice but the voice of us seven, of all of us. "Before we can proceed we must know what you want of us," I said firmly, abject no longer, nor fearful.

Silence received that demand, a throbbing silence behind whose veil I sensed that there was communication among the five who loomed high above us in that aureate niche. And then the voice of the Kintat was replying.

"Of you, Elijah," I sensed it to say, "we want the secret of Faith. We want to know what it was that sustained your kith through centuries of oppression, what it was that moved a certain Man of your people to pay with His agony for the sins of generations yet unborn."

"Of you, Francois Villon, we want the secret of Beauty. We want to know how, with words laid together in a certain order, with sound vibrations combined in certain simple relations, with color and with shape, some among our ancestors could recreate in men born long after they had died their own ecstasy, an ecstasy whose very nature we do not understand.

"Of you, Arthur Pendragon, we want the secret of Obligation. We want to know why you inspired a devotion in those you ruled that transcended all selfish motives. We want to know why, having the power over your people that this devotion gave you, you yet used that power for their welfare and their happiness rather than for your own ends.

"Of you, John Orth, we want the secret of Loyalty. We want to know why, when your prince and friend had slain himself at Mayerling and in no manner could reproach you, you yet gave up all the honors and the luxuries that were yours to carry to some undivulged destination a casket with which he entrusted you, for some purpose you never learned. Because of that something you called loyalty you became a wanderer on the face of the earth. What is there in you that made it impossible for you to do otherwise?"

As I have said, the voice we heard was the voice of all the Kintat, yet, in some way that I did not quite understand, each of the divisions of this long speech seemed to be the contribution of a different Doctil. It had been the one in the center, I later learned he was called Bolar, who had spoken of Faith, Daster of Beauty, Gohret of Obligation. Favril, between Gohret and Bolar, had been the one to question Orth concerning Loyalty. Now it was the turn of Astaris, and his demand was very simply put.

"Of you, John March and Evelyn Rand, we want the secret of Love."

I heard Eve gasp at that, and felt her press even closer to me than she had been. My arm already was about her, so that I did not know whether it was she or I who had brought that about, but beside us there was a soft chuckle that could come only from Villon.

It would amuse a Frenchman, that!

In the next instant my attention was back to the voice, and now it was once more that of the whole Kintat. "We have attained all knowledge. There is not one smallest Law of the Universe which we have not mastered. We know the rules that govern the interaction of Galaxy with Nebula, of proton with neutron and the interplay of all the vast range of entities between. We know the Laws that bind all into one organic whole. Nothing in Nature has any mystery for us, and we have learned that everything in Nature exists and is governed by rigid, immutable laws. We know all —"

"You know not the Eternal, O Benighted!" Elijah's resonant tones flung at them. "You know not God, and without you know Him, you know nothing."

"Precisely, prophet. The laws which govern these five things we do not yet know: Faith, Beauty, Obligation, Loyalty and Love. But their nature also we can learn, in the same manner that we have learned all else, by studying those entities which manifest them. We have found them neither in the stars nor in the ultimate atom, but in you we find them and you shall give us their key."

"When," I responded quietly, "and only when we know *why* you are so anxious to find out about them."

"But that speaks of itself, Monsieur Marsh," the Dauphin's boyish tones broke in. "Is it not that the more understanding a savant acquires, the greater is his thirst to learn more? These creatures here have of knowledge all but these small fragments and it is their nature to not restl till they have fitted the final bits into their picture. There," proudly, "I have solved for you the problem."

I groaned. With one impetuous splutter of his tongue the youngster had stultified everything I had been trying to accomplish. He had supplied the Kintat with a good, a sufficient reason for their demands —

"Remember, my old," Villon whispered. "Truth is their religion. They cannot lie."

"Bless you," I said huskily. And then, "Is that true, Doctils of the Kintat? Is it merely the desire to fill out the last gaps in your view of the Universe that inspires you?"

The response was long in coming. But it came at last, reluctant. "No, John March. We have a definite need for understanding of Faith, Beauty, Obligation, Loyalty and Love."

"What is it? What need have you of these secrets?"

Once more that sense of reluctance, of inaudible consultation among them. Once more the exultant awareness that I had won my point.

"We shall answer you. But it would take too long to set the answer forth in words. Therefore you shall learn it without words."

At that the golden light in the lofty niche above us faded and utter blackness possessed the wall. Possessed not only the wall but that whole vast space and us, a blackness that thumbed my eyes and lay thick against my skin and choked me, so absolute it was.

It was a blackness of non-being. And yet within it there was a stir as of infinitely vast masses moving, and the rush of great winds, and the rumbling thunders of many waters.

"I'm afraid," Eve quavered, close to my ear. "Oh, Johnny, I'm terribly afraid."

CHAPTER 17

DESTINY

A FLECK OF LIGHT FLOWERED IN THE heart of utter light-lessness. Then the light was the Sun, and about the shining orb danced midgelike the spheres of its planets, and the backdrop for them was the whole vast, gold-speckled panoply of the heavens.

Now you must remember that we had no scale of distance or direction by which to measure the tremendous drama now begin-ning. To say we viewed it is really incorrect. *Experienced* is more nearly the proper term, though this too does not quite convey the manner by which it became part of our consciousness.

Perhaps it progressed on a screen before us. Perhaps it moved wholly within our brains, as a dream does. Perhaps within the plasma of our component cells ancestral memories were awakened, and pre-memories (I know no better word) of events yet to be; events implicit in each cell of ours as they were implicit in the microscopic proto-plasm that first blindly stirred with life within the primal deep. How-ever it was, we seemed to be of that which passed in the same manner that humanity itself was of it, not as individuals but as the race itself.

This is as clear an explanation as I can make. It is as clear as it was to me and the others when the final terrible realization burst upon us, and once more we were ourselves. Only the dreadful thing we had learned was clear then, not how we had learned it.

At any rate, there was the Sun, and there its wheeling planets, and we looked upon them as a god might. The next instant a sea, warm and gray and limitless, heaved sluggishly on a green-scummed shore and out upon that shore we crawled, a fish that somehow had gained the ability to breathe.

Hot was the sun, and steamy the air with vapors, and the great, fronded ferns everlastingly dripped moisture on the oozy slime they feathered. So like our own native brine was that climate that we flour-ished and multiplied.

The land heaved as the sea had heaved. Red-glowing rock split its covering of lush black mud, here to be cooled by the hot air that was frigid to its own infernal temperature, there to flow, moving land-scapes of molten fire, into the hissing waters. Many of us perished, but some survived when at last the land froze in the shape it was to hold for aeons.

Legless, scaled creatures we were then, but within us there were mute, inchoate strivings. These gave us blurred sight, and a sort of hearing, and the power to make small, peeping sounds. Some of us thrust out limbs, and some of us learned to carry our progeny within our bodies til they were miniature replicas of ourselves and more fitted to survive in the inimical world.

Now it was cold that threatened our existence, great moving mountains of solid cold that crept indomitably down upon us, pinching us between their groaning walls of death, so that only in a narrow zone was life possible, and there only in a sluggish and dormant way. The ice retreated, and those of us who were left reawakened and the changes to our forms resumed, adapting us to the changes in our habitat. We were furred now, and toothed. Some of us rose erect, and the shapes of our forelimbs changed so that we could swing chattering from limb to limb in the tops of the trees that now cloaked the earth.

We learned that with sticks we could lengthen our reach to secure things that otherwise we might not. We learned that when the overarching foliage failed to shield us from the rains we could find shelter in the caves. We learned that we could soften the rocky floors of the caves and fashion many needed things out of the reeds and out of the mud of the swamps.

In the swamps were monstrous beasts that stalked us for food as we stalked other beasts smaller than ourselves. When we saw the fearful creatures looming upon us, terror wrenched sounds from us and these sounds were always the same. When we heard them we knew they meant danger, and we would flee. After a while we would make these sounds intentionally as warning to others of our kind, even when we who made them were safe.

This worked so well that we set other meanings to other sounds, and no longer had we to rely on gestures alone to convey our groping thoughts.

Because of our own hunting, and because of the hunting of the greater beasts, the small creatures upon which we lived grew sparse. It became a question of which would survive, the giant beasts or us; and since we were so puny we seemed to be doomed. But it dawned on us that though singly we were helpless against them, if we fought against them in hordes we were often triumphant.

To help us in our fight against the giant beasts we devised nets of the vines that everywhere grew luxuriant, and shaped stones and fastened them to the ends of sticks that they might the more dexterously be handled. Yet were we still inept and clumsy in our common endeavours, interfering with one another,l til we ceded to one of us, the strongest first, afterwards the wisest, command over us in our raids.

Hunting together we came to dwell together, and it was natural to obey the chief huntsman in all things. Because he was the greatest among us, his was the right to first choice of meat, and the dryest cave, and the most desirable among our females.

Sometimes one among us disputed the right of another to be chief, and the horde would divide, some cleaving to the one, some to the other. Then would we tear and rend one another with fang and with claw, and with our axes and knives of sharpened flint,l till only one of the parties remained, and the dispute was thus settled.

Sometimes there would be poor hunting in the land where we dwelt and it would be decided to find some other land. Sometimes that other land would be inhabited by some other clan who did not wish to give it up, and so it was necessary to fight with theml till they were slain or enslaved. If our own land was most desirable it was natural that some other tribe should covet it and attempt to wrest it from us. Thus we learned that any men who were different in appearance from us, or whose speech-sounds were not the same as ours, were by these very signs our enemies, to be destroyed if we were in greater force than they, to be fled from if they were the more numerous or the more subtle.

There were these enemies to fear, and there were the beasts to fear, the sabre-toothed tiger, the great snakes of the jungle. But there were things in the world more greatly to be feared than these. There was the great maw that nightly swallowed the sun and that some morning might not disgorge it. There was the recurring winter-death of the world from which we were never sure it would awaken. There were invisible beings who rumbled monstrously in the skies and hurled jagged spears of blue fire down upon us. There were the unseen wraiths of the dark who made men's limbs like water, and heated their blood till it was liquid flame in their veins, and stole away their minds.

Luckily there were among us some who could hold converse with these dread beings, and who could placate them. More powerful than the chiefs became the medicine men, for they could call upon the unseen to destroy the chiefs, and the chiefs feared them.

We learned many things. We learned how to make fire, and how to use it to warm us, and to make more palatable our foods, and to melt certain stones so that they became at once malleable and harder so that from them we could fashion for ourselves better weapons and tools and vessels for cooking and storage. We learned how to go upon the waters, and to journey far from sight of the land, and we found other lands and other peoples to conquer. Our tribes became nations; our chiefly, kings; our medicine men, priests.

Our ways changed, but one way did not change. If men differed from us in language or appearance, they were our enemies and it was our right to take from them that which they possessed and we desired, though we had to destroy or enslave them.

Our knowledge and our skills grew. We changed the face of the earth to suit our desires. We harnessed the lightning to our purpose and laced the continents with roads of stone and of steel. We builded ourselves magnificent cities. We conquered the air and projected our sight and our thought into the farthermost reaches of the heavens. We shifted the atoms at will, making new and ever new compounds.

We bickered and fought among ourselves as we had when we wore skins for clothing and prowled the lush jungle. The wealth we had created we destroyed with a passion and a savagery transcending that of the jungle-men we once were, as the weapons we now used transcended our ancient flint-axes.

Where once a war might involve two tribes or two nations and few hundred square miles of territory, wars now raged over a continent, a hemisphere, over all the globe. Where once only the men of a nation battled in set lines behind which there were hunger and distress but at least no peril to limb and life, now crashing bombs and deadly gases rained out of the sky and our women and children, our aged and crippled were engulfed in the holocaust.

As war after war spawned new and more terrible instruments of mass murder, in the intervals between wars we would attempt the formation of some world organization that would put an end to war. Each such league would be born with the same high hopes, each would be born with the same cancer; the reluctance of every nation to yield what was called its 'sovereignty.' Sometimes indeed, so dreadful were the weapons that the last war had evolved, it appeared that rather than bring upon the world the universal destruction they promised, the nations would yield as much as was required of this 'sovereignty.' But always in the end the scientists of one nation or another would devise a defence, or what they thought was a defence, against the latest avatar of death or perhaps would secretly invent a new and more terrible one, and the latest League of Peace would die.

Triumph for one side or the other, or exhaustion of both sides, would end a war, and such was our indomitable spirit that we would turn back at once to the arts of peace. Science all but conquered disease and began even to find ways of combatting the slow deterioration of senility so that our life span grew always longer.

Through the ravages of war and our other careless dealing with natural resources, the area of tillable land kept lessening. But biologists discovered how to grow our vegetable foods with their roots in liquid plasma of inorganic salts that filled enormous trays, piled high in gigantic tiered structures.

Domestic animals, too, were bred in factories rather than on farms. Huge sheds of steel these were, miles long; their one end alive with the bawling of cattle, the cackling of hens, the baaing of sheep, the other shaking with the hammer and pound of the slaughtering and dressing machines; pouring forth the products of an agriculture that had become a mechanized industry.

These agricoles were built near the cities whose population they fed; and so, there being no longer need for any of us to live separated from our fellows, we gathered together in the cities. These grew infinitely vaster than we could have conceived in the Twentieth Century; but where there were no cities the wilderness reclaimed its own, cloaking with tangled greenery the unpeopled land.

Mile upon mile the cities stretched, great masses of concrete and steel. Many-levelled they were, covered over against the elements by monstrous shells, lighted no longer by the Sun, but by a cold and sourceless artificial light that never lessened and never brightened.

The cities breathed air held to an even temperature, moistened to the optimum degree, dustless and germless. Within them were the teeming warrens where we dwelt; the throbbing, thunderous factories where we labored; arenas for such sports as our thinning blood permitted us to partake in; theatres and music halls. Threading the cities in soaring arabesques were the street-ways, trafficless because their paving itself moved, slowly at the outer margins, swifter and more swiftly towards the center. Always the Ways were crowded, for there was no longer day or night for us but only the work and rest and sleep periods that the Aristos decreed.

The Aristos were the brain of our body politic, the Leaders and Masters of men. Obsolete as the chiefs of the ancient clans had become kings and presidents, outmoded as the fire-centered tribal Councils were parliaments and congresses. Forgotten except by some wild-eyed anachronisms was the quaint idea that the State exists to serve its people, a contention as fantastic as that a human body exists to serve the cells of which it is composed.

The State, we had learned, was the be-all and end-all of life, each citizen subordinate to its weal. Each contributed to the State the best that he was able, each received from the State a recompense measured by what he contributed.

Centuries of leadership, of training had endowed the Aristos with their innate genius for management, their congenital fitness to govern. They were the incarnation of the State, their decrees its laws, their will, its will. They regulated our every act, set our every task, dictated our every thought, ruled all the minutiae of our lives so that the State might best be served.

It was their due, was it not, that they should be rewarded with every luxury the civilization they created could produce? Was it not their right to have first choice of all the best of life, even though the Plebos were by millions the more numerous?

The Plebos carried out the behests of the Aristos, serving the State and grateful that by being of use to the State they earned the right to live at all. Cast by birth in a grosser mould, they were fit only to give to the State their labor in time of peace, their bodies when war flared between the cities.

Not that their labor was long or arduous. For this we had to thank the Doctors of Learning, the Doctils.

A caste apart were the Doctils. Like the Plebos they were amenable to the Aristos, but their rewards in luxury of living were but little, if at all, inferior to those which accrued to the Masters themselves.

Magnificent were the Doctils' contributions to the State; in machines that did all the world's work under the unremittent attendance of the Plebos; in knowledge that probed the Universe for new ways to exalt the State. They gave us stratcars that shuttled above earth's atmosphere and brought the farthest distant of our cities within an hour's journey. They gave us spaceships that visited Mars and Venus and fetched for us new and strange elements to make more godlike our life. They fashioned for us our brave, new world.

It was the Doctils who made the State the efficient mechanism it had become. Take, for instance, the matter of human procreation.

By the old, biological process, a full half of the Plebos, the females, were incapacitated for their usual employment during the recurring periods of gestation. This was, of course, a direct loss to the common weal, but the disturbance to the State's economy did not end with that. Since the only limits to life now were those set by war, and infrequent accident, there were times when no additions to our population were required, others when great numbers of Plebos were badly needed. But, utterly obedient to the decrees of the Aristos as they were in all else, the Plebos could not be regimented in their mating habits. This situation seriously threatened the meticulous balance of work and workers that had been set up, and posed economic problems not even the genius of the Aristos could solve.

The scientists changed all that in a single brilliant stroke. They devised a method by which ova were removed from the human body, artificially fertilized, and kept in a state of suspended animation until such time as additions to the population were required. When the need arose, by various ingenious processes the maturation of the stored eggs was brought about at twenty times the previous rate, so that within one year exactly the desired number of new Plebos at the efficient age were produced. Thus it became possible to sterilize all male Plebos, and all but the comparatively small number of females required to supply the basic ova. Thereafter, by certain treatment of the growing embryos; only neuter Plebos were matured, except for the few females, the Matras, required to replace those who for one reason or another ceased to function.

The Aristos directed that the Doctils apply the process to their own class as well as to the Plebos, but exempted themselves from it. Their superior self-discipline, they proclaimed, rendered it needless as far as they were concerned.

Oddly enough, the Doctils argued against this decree, maintaining that they did not fall behind the Aristos in self-discipline. But their appeal was denied, and there was nothing for them but to obey, since all the weapons they had invented — the disintegrating rays, the atom bombs, the sonic vibrators that changed the frequency of nervous impulses till those upon whom they were focused became insane — were entirely in the hands of the Aristos and none knew better than the scientists how futile opposition to them would be.

So dreadful, indeed, were these weapons, that no City any longer dared to make war upon another, and we knew peace at last had come to Earth.

For some centuries we occupied ourselves with the business of living. To the Plebos it was a dreary business, because they were cogs in machines that ran smoothly and without vibration and without purpose, unless that purpose were to provide luxury for the Aristos.

The Doctils occupied themselves with the pursuit of ultimate knowledge, and with many curious experiments, such as that of changing our shape and form in better adaptation to the tasks set for us. The Aristos were amused by the results of these trials, and mildly interested in the discoveries the Doctils made as they probed even farther into the infinite and infinitesimal, but mostly they were engrossed in their own sybaritic pleasures, pleasures neither Doctils nor Plebos any longer could comprehend.

How could the sexless understand dalliance between male and female? How could those whose very bodies had been changed so that they were fit only for their assigned function in the economy of the State understand beauty of sound or color or form? How could those whose every act was meshed into the acts of those about them in absolute and rigid cooperation understand the joy of competitive sport?

Somewhere in these centuries the Doctils learned how to transmute energy into matter, so that no longer was it needful for our ships to ply space, nor our stratcars to dart across the skies in trade between the Cities.

This was a consummation welcomed by us. The people of each city spoke different languages, differed from one another in color, in cephalic formation, in bony structure; hence they were natural enemies. As long as we had been mutually interdependent for the unique resources of our contiguous territories, we had been forced to maintain a certain basis for more or less peaceful intercourse. Now the need for this was done away with. It took only a brief conference of the Aristos of the world to decide upon a complete severance of relations. The City shells were ordered permanently sealed against entrance or exit and now each City was a world unto itself, completely self-sufficient.

Man himself at last was completely self-sufficient, wholly independent of Nature, wholly independent of all but his own powers. Two million years after the first lunged fish crawled out of a steamy sea, Mankind had reached its apogee.

"BUT THEY DENY JEHOVAH!" a sonorous voice thundered across the heavens. "THEY SPURN THE ETERNAL. BEHOLD! THEY HAVE TURNED THEIR FACES FROM GOD AND HE HAS TURNED HIS FACE FROM THEM AND LACKING HIS COUNTENANCE THEY MUST PERISH."

CHAPTER 18

THE CURTAIN FALLS

I was vaguely aware that it was Elijah who had thus broken into the tremendous drama of Man's Destiny. As vaguely I was aware of the others who shared with me this experience, but it seemed to me that someone was missing.

"There is neither nobility nor chivalry among them." Arthur's voice was something heard half dreaming, half waking. "Their rulers govern only for themselves without obligation to their subjects . . ." It was all dim and unreal but quite clearly there were six of us, not seven, as Orth's deep accents rumbled, "Nothing but machines they are and like machines they work only how and as long as they are ordered. There is not one who is loyal to his task or to another. Not one . . ."

Evelyn was phantasmal, but wraithlike as she was there still was a thrill for me in her bated whisper. "How terrible, Johnny. How very terrible. There is no love in that world, no one to love . . ."

They were shimmering back into the blackness; Elijah, Arthur, Louis, John Orth. Evelyn was fading as the blackness closed in; but where was Villon! He had not spoken of the absence of Beauty from the drear world of Man's future. He was gone from among us.

Was he only the first to go? Were we to vanish one by one while those who remained were engrossed in this pageant of Man's Destiny? The blackness became absolute again.

Once more we were part of the colossal drama, of the cosmic tragedy that moved swiftly — now and inevitably to its final curtain.

Man had attained the ultimate. Within the sealed shells of the Cities we had achieved perfection.

Between the Cities spread a dark and whispering wilderness. Through the gloomy forest aisles of the Wastelands prowled wild beasts that had changed but little from those that we had hunted — and feared — in the dim and shadowed past. Out there the winds still seethed through rustling leaves, streams still babbled down to an untracked sea, and the sun still shone, but none of this had any meaning for us.

'Til, in Moska, farthest north of the Cities, the Plebos in charge of the climate machines noted that these were speeding up beyond any rate known before in their effort to warm to the thermostatically predetermined degree the air drawn, through immense ducts, from outside the shell.

In accordance with regulations, this curious circumstance was reported to the Aristos of Moska. These ordered their Doctils to investigate.

The Doctils checked the climate machines and found nothing wrong with them. Their peculiar performance must be due to an unprecedented drop in the temperature of the Wasteland air. The scientists made some adjustments in the machines and requested permission of the Aristos to break the seals of the City shell, so that they might determine just what changes were occurring outside.

This permission the Aristos denied. The Doctils, they argued, were trying to cover up some mistake of their own, or perhaps were even involved in some conspiracy against the State. This accusation they held proven when the scientists took the unprecedented step of persisting in their plea and dared even to hint that the Aristos were something less than all-wise. The matter was settled out of hand by a mass execution of all the Doctils of Moska. They were, after all, no longer needed since Man had attained perfection.

The Aristos returned to their pleasures. The Plebos continued functioning in the rhythmic routine of their labors. Nothing had changed. Nothing except that the climate machines continued speeding up.

Then the enclosing shell of Moska commenced to groan under some inexplicable pressure from without.

For the first time in memory, the Plebos were aware of an emotion — that of apprehension. But habit confined them inexorably to their routine, and it was the Aristos, themselves breaking the seals, who discovered that Moska was doomed.

Mountains of ice, an endless continent of it, were moving down from the Pole to swamp the City! It was possible that Doctils might have devised some means of dissipating the ice or forcing it back, but there were no longer any Doctils in Moska. As matters stood, there was no recourse but to abandon the City before its human occupants were ground to pulp in the ruin of its soaring structures.

The advance of the glacier, inevitable though it was, was infinitely slow and the shell was very strong, so there was time to prepare an orderly evacuation while messengers were dispatched in hastily reconditioned stratcars to arrange for accommodation by the Cities of Berl, Par and Lond, Moska's nearest neighbors.

Meantime, the far southern City of Melbour was commencing to have difficulties with its own climate machines. These were as yet, however, not serious enough to be alarming.

There was a great deal of confusion in Moska. The Plebos, wrenched from their accustomed tasks, were bewildered. The

Aristos, deprived of the guidance of the Doctils, were not at all certain as to just what should be done, or how. There was, however, nothing approaching panic until the stratcars returned with their reports.

These were all three alike. Each crew had had trouble in penetrating the shells of the Cities to which they had been sent. When they had succeeded in this and delivered their plea, the answer in each case had been an immediate and incontinent refusal.

"Moska's predicament is no concern of ours," the Aristos of Lond, for example, had replied. "We see no reason to upset the balanced economy of our State on behalf of strangers."

The consternation with which these reports were received was followed by boiling wrath, and then a grim determination. "What they will not give us," was the decision, "we shall take."

A rending crash, the first crack of the shell, emphasized the need for haste. Before the Great Glacier had advanced another meter, the sky was darkened with a vast cloud of stratcars and rocket-ships, crewed with Plebos, captained by Aristos.

The destruction of Moska was earth-shaking thunder in the north as its fleets swept toward Berl and Par and Lond.

But these were not taken by surprise. They had sent spies on the trail of the homing Moskvites to verify the truth of their tales, and these had sounded the warning. Up from the threatened Cities leaped their own myriad-numbered fleets and the enemies met fifty miles high over the Wastelands.

An Inferno took possession of the startled silences of the substratosphere; a hell of lancing, lethal beams, of crepitating ionic discharges; a cataclysmic Hades of sounds that invaded men's brains and set them mad.

Across the heavens that prodigious battle raged, and the heavens were a sheet of flame out of which rained soot that had been men, and white-glowing embers that moments before had been proud, space-eating ships and fleet stratcars. The forests received this dust-hail of destruction, and the heat of the disrupted atoms set fire to the forests, and the flame above was matched by the searing spread of flame below.

For a little space the remnants of those mighty fleets still fought, and that little while was sufficient to complete the contagion of disaster. While the darting ion-lances of the cosmic annihilators, the radioactive blasts of the atom bombs, and the beams of the disintegrators obeyed the laws of ethereal vibration and sped off into outer space in straightline tangents from Terra's globe, the maddening shrills of the sonic vibrators were conducted to Earth's surface by its atmosphere, were carried to the Cities not as yet involved in the explosion. High pitched and fiendish, they penetrated the shells of Madri and of Byzant, of Ning and Tok and Nyork, and curdled the brains of the Aristos and Doctils and Plebos that dwelt there.

The madness seized upon all of us who heard those sounds, and none of us escaped. We were stripped of all that the centuries had taught us, were left only with what we had learned in the steamy jungles in whose treetops we had swung chattering, in the caves where we had shivered with fear of the beasts and hate for alien men ingrained itself in the germinal genes of our race. *The hordes were* on *the* move! The enemy hordes were swooping down upon us! If we did not kill them they would kill us.

Kill! Kill! KILL! *KILL!*

From Losan and Washton, from Alexan and Buenos and Capetin, burst our fleets to hurricane across the world, seeking those of alien speech and alien countenance who because they were different from us needs must be our enemies.

We found one another in the screaming empyrean, we found those who sought us as we sought them, and we shattered together with the crash of our atom bombs and the lightnings of our disintegrators and the lunatic shriek of our sirens.

Now the skies were a fury of death, and the face of the Earth was a seething conflagration and the madness that wailed, "kill, kill, KILL," ringed the spinning sphere where Man had achieved the ultimate. The ultimate in self-destruction, for nowhere on that blazing orb, nowhere in the incandescent atmosphere enveloping it, could life longer exist.

There were no victors in that last war of all, and there were no vanquished; for when the fires had burned themselves out Earth was a dead planet, its flesh of soil blasted and torn and blackened, its bones of rock melted into the tortured, nightmare skeleton of that which had been the Sun's most favored child.

There could be no life left on such an Earth, but all Earth-life was not extinct.

CHAPTER 19

THE WILL TO LIVE AND KILL

IF, SOME CENTURIES BACK, THE Aristos had not included the Doctils in the Law of Controlled Procreation, the Story of Mankind would now be ended.

Although they had ventured some feeble protest, the Doctils of the world had accepted the edict — except for a certain one in Moska.

This one, Roya by name, had been perhaps the last human alive who did not altogether subscribe to the doctrine of the State Supreme and to the omniscience and omnipotence of the Masters.

Roya resented the Aristos' act, resented even more his fellow scientists acquiescence therewith. He became definitely non-social. Hereafter, he decided, he would share his accomplishments with no one. He would, moreover, direct his researches toward the discovery of hitherto unknown natural laws, and new applications of known laws, that would enable him eventually to gain control of Moska, and then of the world, for himself.

Benefitting by the pooling of the thought of all the other Doctils of the City while withholding the bulk of his own scientific achievements, Roya forged far ahead of the rest of the fellowship of the Doctils. He learned that beyond the identity of matter and energy was a more fundamental identity of pure thought with both, and that this was the true reality. He learned the nature of Time; that the Past and the Future coexist with the Present, and he learned how to move pastward along Time's flux, though he did not quite solve the problem of how to take himself futureward. He learned how to warp Space at will, so that at will he could place himself instantaneously at any point in its infinity.

So many avenues of speculation did his discoveries open up that even Roya's great brain faltered at the task of exploring them all. He required aid, but he dared not communicate his knowledge and his intentions to any man. They would without any measure of doubt be reported at once to the Aristos, and these would at once move to purge him. He was not yet quite ready for a test of his powers, not yet quite sure that single-handed he could defeat a world.

His dilemma he solved thus: He brought about an accident in which a score or so of Plebos were killed. When the maturation of a sufficient number of fertilized ova to replace them was commenced, Roya managed to be assigned to the task and contrived to abstract from the storage trays five additional eggs. The nutrient baths in which these were placed he secretly adjusted so that they would mature as Doctils possessed of all his own store of knowledge and with his own non-social psychology.

In a year Roya would have help in his great project, five Doctils who would not betray him. But Roya did not live quite to the end of that year. He was one of the scientists purged when the first premonition of the Glacier brought about the dispute between them and the Aristos.

The interval between that incident and the departure of the Moskvite fleets for their attack on their neighboring Cities was just about sufficient for the five to reach their full growth. Completely armed with their foster-father's omniscience, they were at once aware of the implications of what was occurring and knew instantly what they must do to escape the catastrophe. The general confusion made it easy for them to seize Moska's largest spaceship, kill its Aristo officers and get it safely away from Earth before the sonic vibrators commenced spreading their contagion of madness. Within our spaceship now were all that remained of Man: we five newfledged Doctils, our ship's crew of a hundred Plebos and a single Matra, an egg-bearing female that Daster had had the inspiration to include in our cargo.

Included in that freight was also a complete assortment of the various devices our civilization had produced, so that our vessel was a microcosmic City as self-contained and as self-sufficient as any of those that now had been blasted into nonexistence. In a manner that with his inability to travel into the Future Roya could not have foreseen we who owed our existence to him had absolute dominion over the destiny of our race.

"It is," Bolar thought to us, "as if this ship were the germinal cell from which a new and greater civilization will evolve."

"Aye," sighed Daster. "But where? See. Earth is now a whirling cinder, heated by the fires of its immolation."

"It will cool," Favril reminded him.

"It will cool," Astaris agreed. "And then the ice will form again at the Poles, and creep down once more over the blackened desolation till the grinding masses meet at the Equator. A thousand years, and more, it will be before they once more retreat. A thousand years — Do we wish to wait that long before we rebuild our home?"

Favril had a suggestion. "There are the other planets, brothers. Mars, Perhaps, or Venus —"

"Neither," Gohret interrupted, "will support life in the form we know it."

"Then we can change our form of life," Favril argued, "to meet the conditions on either." But he himself was halfhearted in advancing the idea, and none thought it necessary to voice the veto all agreed upon.

Our head-membranes throbbed with an adumbration of despair and in the brains of more than one of us there was a flicker of something not quite thought suggesting that it might be best to flash our ship and all it contained into oblivion. But there is a Natural Law that compels every entity to cling to the preservation of its kind.

"I have it!" Daster's thought-waves impacted on our receptors. "There is no place for us in the Solar System, nor in the Galaxy of which it is a part. But somewhere among the myriads upon myriads of planetary bodies with which Space is filled, somewhere between infinity and infinity, must be another orb upon which the conditions are enough like Terra's for it to afford us shelter. Let us find it, brothers!"

"Let us find it!" our minds took up the cry, and at once we were projecting ourselves through the endless reaches of the Universe in such a search as even Roya would have been hard put to it to conceive.

Beyond Pluto, beyond Andromeda, beyond Suns whose light would have taken a billion years to reach us, we probed the Universe. Not in actuality. That monumental exploration of ours carried not one proton of us beyond the walls of our rocketship. It was mathematical, our hunt for a home for the life that was in our charge. It was a matter of unreeling countless formulae, of tracing countless curves, of an infinity of calculations based upon the infinity of data we had been born possessed of through the genius of our fosterfather, Roya.

And when it was ended, the result was this: Nowhere in the Universe was there any orb duplicating exactly the conditions on Terra. Only one planet, a million galaxies away, would support life in anything like the form we wished to preserve it. Only one.

It was Bolar whose calculations lit upon this. We checked, rechecked, his figures and found them faultless.

"We know where we want to go," Gohret summed it up. "Let us go there." But we still hesitated, gazing upon devastated Earth, upon white blazing Sun and its attendant planets wheeling about it, upon the golden constellations that we were about to leave forever. Though in point of personal life we were but hours old, compact within us were the history and the memories of our race; and these whirling orbs, these spangled skies, were the very warp and woof of our being.

Something held us, some inchoate and wordless nostalgia unworthy of creatures of perfect science, of perfect mind, such as we were.

"Let us go." Gohret the implacable recalled us to our task.

None of us had actually warped space to translate himself across it, but we knew how it must be done and we knew that it must be done just so or irretrievable disaster would overtake us. The disaster of a timeless, spaceless state of being, of a non-existence that was yet existence; endless, hopeless, the incarnation of eternal despair.

Five of us there were, and a hundred Plebos and one Matra, and we were all that was left of Man. One minutest error in what we were about to do would end humankind forever.

We set the proper forces at work in the proper manner.

Then —

Grayness. Non-being absolute. Non-knowledge. Only a terrible fear, a terrible certainty, that the error had been made and we were doomed eternally to this cognizant oblivion.

Our spaceship, the hundred and six of us within it, hung motionless at the upper limit of a sunless, brown sky such as no Man had ever viewed. Below was a quarter sphere of the planet we had traversed the Galaxies to seek and we knew at once that life was possible upon it, because there *was* life upon it.

What we could see of the world to which we had come was a level plain from over whose horizon stalked colonnades of pastel-hued, immense pillars that converged at its center on a mountain black and lustreless as the starless wastes between the nebulae. The wide paths set off by these roofless palisades, close-packed with the planet's denizens, seemed straight-banked dark rivers flowing toward the stygian pile that focussed them, and from those marching myriads a tidal wave of cadenced sound welled up to us.

A chorus of countless voices, the paean was yet a single, harmonious whole. There was solemnity to it, and awe, yet there was to it also joy and an exceeding ecstasy.

We could not read the meaning of that hymn. The meaning was not thought but an *emotion* that held those thousands upon thousands in a single thrall, and Earthman had so long ago discarded emotion that its very nature was forgotten. But we knew that it was inspired by the monstrous black mountain —

It was no mountain, or rather it was a mountain carved into a stupendous image of a hooded Being neither man nor beast, but transcending both.

It was not the image itself to which the emotion vocalised by a world's song was directed, but that which it depicted; not in form, because the Being had no form, but in representation of Its attributes. This much, gazing upon it, we could understand, but what those attributes were we could not comprehend, nor how any living race could worship them as this one did.

Curiously enough, we were aware that if we held our attention upon that monument for more than a brief instant, or longer permitted ourselves to hear the organ tones welling about us, we should be unable to do that which we had come to do. So at once we ordered our Plebos to the armament of our ship and they loosed their bolts upon the singing masses below.

The plain heaved in a vast shattering. The splendid, tall pillars collapsed upon the worshippers who had marched between them singing and now screamed their terror at the sudden destruction that came upon them without warning. No hymn now, but shrieks, shrilled through the crashing chaos of a world disrupted, through the rending of rock whose very atoms were being smashed into their component atoms, through he pealing thunders of the doom we had hurled upon them.

A cloud of dust rose out of the slaughter, and enveloped the orb below us. The cloud was luminous with the greens and scarlets and blinding blues of our armament, and it was black with the agony it concealed . . .

"*Cruel*. Oh, cruel." Eve's horrified whisper lay somewhere within the heart of that terrible spectacle. "They are not men, they're glorified beasts, Johnny. It can't be that this is what the years will make of people like you and me!"

Enough of my own personality had shimmered back that I might have answered her, but I did not. I could only have reminded her of fiery destruction raining from Twentieth Century skies on screaming women, and little children, on humans guiltless and unwarned kneeling at prayer in the cathedrals of their faith . . .

It was not our intention to destroy that race entirely, not at least until we could determine whether they might in some manner be of use to us and so we ordered our weapons shut off while still there was some evidence of life below. One disintegrator, throttled to minimum power, we used to sweep the veiling vapors out of the atmosphere.

The plain was a vast tumulus of rocky shards piled helter-skelter. The singing thousands were dissipated into their primal atoms, so that it was as if they had never been, but here and there gray-purple masses heaved in shocked and aimless movement.

The monument rose from that desert of desolation, its configuration altered hardly at all. Its miles-long body was still haunched as it had been, its great head poised neckless on gargantuan shoulders as before the holocaust.

Not quite as before. It must be because some fragments had been riven from it, that it seemed to have moved slightly, so that the hooded eyes appeared now to be directed towards us, hanging high above.

There was a sudden coldness within us, a sudden incomprehensible something that might be fear. And yet we sensed no anger in that veiled, quiet glance, no menace. Only a waiting, endlessly patient.

Strange, then, that in our moment of triumph, in the moment that we had proved ourselves masters of the universe and of all Life, we should be afflicted by this curious Unease.

CHAPTER 20

CHOICE BETWEEN DEATH AND DEATH

OUR ATTENTION RETURNED TO THOSE that were left of the planet's animate inhabitants, was returned to them by a wave of cold hostility, of hate and malevolence, of determination to resist us until none of them were left. The wave was thought, the single thought of the masses below that were writhing back to awareness, and we could not tolerate it.

That hate would render them useless to us and we could make use of the drina — so we were aware now they called themselves — as slaves. The problem was easy to solve. We had not yet used our sonic vibrator. We reduced its power and stepped up its frequency till it emitted a whistle just within the threshold of audibility, and we unloosed that whistle on the remnants of the conquered race.

The masses shuddered momentarily, then were still. The drina were mindless now, whatever intelligence they'd possessed destroyed. They were ours to control as we controlled the Plebos we had brought with us, as we controlled the ship whose shell enclosed us.

We zoomed downward to take possession of our new home.

Our attack upon the planet had blasted its surface into a wilderness of tumbled rock and had destroyed all evidence of the *drina's* civilization, but these circumstances exactly suited our purpose. We could fashion a city here that would equal or surpass any that had existed on Earth, and from the ova with which our Matra would supply us we could people it with exactly the form of humanity we desired.

We decided to plan carefully and without haste. We would, for the present, merely construct a temporary abode. Having recuperated from the tremendous drain on our vitality that all we had accomplished had entailed, we would design a Super-State.

Pursuant to this decision, we hollowed out for ourselves a smooth pit as distant from the disturbing black image as we could. From the molten rock with which our disintegrators thus furnished us, we moulded a number of structures to temporarily house ourselves, the freight of our rocketship, the Plebos and the Matra. For some not very well apprehended reason, we designed Adalon on the plan of the Solar System we had abandoned forever.

As matters of reasonable precaution we surrounded the bowl with a Veil of Ishlak, a wall of force impenetrable unless it is opened by controls from within, and assigned certain of the Plebos to roam the lands beyond the Veil, keeping watch on the drina.

Having thus set matters in order, we rested and refreshed ourselves for a space, and then called the first council of our Kintat of Doctils.

"I am aware of a curious feeling of dissatisfaction," Favril opened the council. "Although when I proposed that We remain within the confines of our System, I was compelled to acknowledge that your arguments against it were very cogent, I still feel that I was not altogether wrong."

"In spite of the fact that Bolar's calculations have proved to be correct and we find here a temperature and humidity, a gravity, a range of elements, sufficiently like those of Terra to make it possible for our form of life to exist, I yet sense in the very environment some intangible hostility to Mankind that makes me doubt the success of our experiment."

"What would you have?" Gohret demanded. "A world ready made for us?"

"Precisely," Daster responded. "We abandoned Earth because it is a denuded sphere. Have we anything better here? Is not the same amount of labor required to make this planet tenable as would have been required had we returned to Terra? And there we would have been where we belong."

"That is it!" Favril exclaimed. "That is what troubles me. We do not belong here. We are resented by the very ground, by the very rocks. We have vanquished its inhabitants, but the planet itself rejects us. It is because of this, vaguely realized, that we built Adalon as we did, to comfort us."

Gohret's answer to that was a sneer. "Earth, too, rejected us. Mait's folly completed the catastrophe that ended Man's life on Earth, but a natural phenomenon, the advent of a new Glacial Age, was the spark that initiated the cataclysm. Had Lond and Par and Berl taken us in, still would the ice have advanced, pinching us between its walls, till we should have been obliterated."

"Not so," Daster objected. "Had we not shut ourselves away from Nature, had we kept in touch with it, we should have found a way to avoid disaster. The genius of Man was unconquerable, as long as Man cooperated with Nature and did not war against it."

"The mistake was made," Bolar offered, "when the City shells were sealed —"

"No," Favril cut in. "When the Law of Controlled Procreation was decreed and Man became a designed creation of Man himself."

"We started to go wrong long before that," Bolar ventured. "I think it was when the Agricoles were perfected and men abandoned the good ground for the cities. That was when we definitely turned our back upon natural evolution and —"

"You are all tight, and you are all wrong," Astaris said softly. "All you mention was done because Man had become wholly a thinking machine, had forgotten certain basic urges not susceptible to reason but very necessary to his happiness. Only their names are left to us, their meaningless names. Love. Loyalty. Obligation. Beauty. And Faith. Faith above all."

"All this is futile," Gohret drowned him out, harshly. "What is done, is done. Only what is still to be done concerns us. Our future lies on this planet. We cannot return to the Solar System, to Earth —"

"Ah, but we can," Astaris answered. "We can go back to Earth, and to an Earth renewed and vigorous, fully fitted for the Super-Civilization we intend to erect. We can correct all the errors our predecessors have made."

"How?"

"By returning not only in Space but in *Time* to our native sphere. Here is what I propose. Let us consolidate our position here, but only temporarily. Let us scout all history for those among our ancestors in whom the traits I have mentioned were best developed, bring them here, and probe them for the secrets of those emotions. Having found them, let us adjust the nurture of the new race we are founding to include those traits. This having been done, we can —"

"Select the period of Earth's geological evolution," Gohret snatched the thesis from him, "when natural conditions were most favorable —"

"I've calculated it," Bolar put in. "The Twentieth Century —"

"So long ago!" Favril exclaimed.

"So long ago. That was when the interrelation of Man and Nature was at its best and that was when Man began to gain that ascendancy over Nature that eventually led to his undoing. My figures are irrefutable."

"Very well," Gohret took back the current of thought. "We'll try Astaris' project. When it is successfully terminated, or we find it futile, as I think more probable, we shall return to Earth of the Twentieth Century. We shall take possession of it in the same manner that we have taken possession of this planet, destroy or enslave its denizens, repopulate it with the younglings; we shall create from the ova our Matra bears within her. With our limitless knowledge, our inheritance of two million years of evolution, what wonders shall we not bring to pass! Done, brothers?"

"Done!"

CHAPTER 21

EXPERIMENT IN LOVE

BLACKNESS BLOTTED OUT THAT moment conference of the Kintat, blackness absolute. Within that blackness I was rigid, all my bodily warmth gone, unable to think, aware only that I had heard pronounced the doom of my people, that I had heard sentence passed on it of destruction, immediate and terrible.

I no longer was Man in General, living the history of mankind through the ages. I was John March, lawyer, born June twelfth, nineteen hundred and twenty into a good, green world I loved. It was my New York, my America, that these soulless, ruthless beings intended to seize for their own. It was the boys and girls with whom I had grown up that they were going to destroy or enslave. It was the fellows who'd sweated over our studies with me, who'd chased a pigskin up and down the field beside me. It was the one-armed newsdealer on the corner, and the people who jostled me in the subway, it was Pierpont Alton Sturdevant, and Mary, the pert-nosed telephone girl in the reception room, and the cop who'd handed me a ticket for speeding, whom they would treat as they had treated the drina hymning their God!

Evelyn formed out of the blackness, straight and slender as a naiad, a horror akin to my own graven on her dear face. Arthur and Orth were real again, straddle-legged, their fists clenched on their useless weapons. Louis Capet was a shaking, terrified little boy —

Elijah's right hand was raised above the shaggy, silver crown of his great head. His face was upturned to the high, vaulted roof of the vast nave, and his lips were moving in prayer to the Jehovah who was not there above him, nor anywhere in this space or this time. I heard him. I heard the eternal plaint of his people from his lips, the plaint that was now for me the plaint of all the people of my world and my time. *"My God,"* the sonorous Hebrew rolled from those lips. *"My God, why hast thou forsaken me!"*

But I could see Francois Villon nowhere.

"John March!" It was the inner voice of the Future Man that called my name. "John March!" The goldenlighted niche was visible again in the topless, ebony wall, and within it there was not the five Doctils of the Kintat, but only one! Achronos Astaris! "We have told you what we want of you, and we have shown you why. We have shown you that we had no need to make a bargain with you, and yet, having made it, we have kept it. Now we call upon you and your companions to yield to us that which we desire, promising in exchange to return you to the location in Time and Space from which we brought you here and now."

Somehow I found my voice. "So that we may be destroyed along with the rest?"

"Only you and Evelyn Rand are of the Twentieth Century. The others will live out their span, all memory of their adventure here blotted from their minds."

"And we two?"

"Will also remember nothing, but will die or be enslaved as chance may dictate, when we descend upon your world."

My neck corded, so that for a moment my defiant reply was choked within my throat. In that moment, Eve's hand was on my arm, her taut voice in my ear.

"Our choice is only between death and death, Johnny, and as long as we die together I don't care at all. The others have a real choice. Let them answer."

She was right! I turned to them, my loved one in the circle of one arm. "It's your chance, my friends," I said, smiling. We were set apart from them, Eve and I, but we were one, completely and wholly one, and for that moment nothing else really mattered to me. I had lost hope and life and a world, but I had gained her. Everything after that would be anticlimax. "Take it."

Elijah's dark and brooding eyes came down from communion with the Eternal to fasten on the bizarre creature in the recess. The Dauphin straightened and was no longer a frightened lad, but the scion of a king. Arthur was regal in every line of his great body, his purple robes imperial. Orth was granite-countenanced, expressionless.

Where was Villon?

"What is your answer?" the Doctil demanded, and there was a curious impatience in the way he did so. An odd exigency.

It was Louis' high pipe that sounded first, the thin voice of a little boy. "For myself the answer is — No!"

"And for me," Orth's deep tones echoed him. "No!"

"The devil and all his fiends take you," King Arthur boomed. "Rather than live as poltroons, we choose to die as men!"

The Hebrew prophet was the last, statuesque in his white robes, his hawkbeaked countenance dark as doom. His bearded lips moved. "Ye have abandoned God. Can I give God back to you?"

They had their faults each of these men, the faults of the times and the kinds of humans they represented. Elijah, was the prophet of a creed that could be cruel and relentless, a creed one of whose dogmas was, "An Eye for an Eye, a Tooth for a Tooth." Underlying the magnificent pageantry of King Arthur's Age of Chivalry had been thousands of the disinherited; rags for their clothing, straw for their beds, bones to gnaw for food and unremitting, hopeless toil for their way of life. The Dauphin was the last of a dynasty that had ground and oppressed a nation, without conscience and without mercy. John Orth had been bred in an Imperial Court whose intrigue and chicanery and diplomacy of exploitation was to bring about the first World War and its grim aftermaths.

But Astaris had offered them life, the living out of their lives as those lives were meant to be lived, instead of a grisly death. Neither their world nor their own consciences would know what they had done, nor reproach them for having done it, yet they had the courage and the integrity to refuse him.

When I turned back to Astaris I sensed that he shared my admiration for them. I sensed, too, a certain sadness, a certain disappointment.

"Consider again," he insisted. "Consider that whether or not you give us what we ask, we shall nevertheless possess ourselves of Earth of the Twentieth Century. With or without the knowledge we seek from you, we shall carry out our plan. You cannot stop us."

What I said in reply was inane and without meaning and vainglorious. But I am not sorry I said, "We can try, Astaris. We can try our damndest."

Our damndest would be little indeed against him and his mates, who were masters of a knowledge I could not even attempt to comprehend, but I had to fling that defiance at him and I felt more of a man for having done so.

"Give us strength, Oh Eternal," I heard Elijah behind me, "to endure what it is Thy will we shall endure." Then Arthur's voice was booming, "Have at him brothers. Take him for hostage!" and the huge, purple-robed form was surging past me, *Excalibur* flashing above its flowing blonde locks. Orth pounded beside Arthur, and beside Orth the boy ran, lithe and pantherlike.

And I had joined them. It might work! If we could make Astaris our prisoner — "Down, Orth," I cried, still scheming, lawyerlike. "Down on your hands and knees to make a spring-board for us." He went down as I said, at the base of the wall, and Arthur was leaping from his back for the niche, and had made it. Louis bounded high, reached the recess. My own feet felt John Orth's back. My knees bent, straightened, threw me in such a jump as I'd never yet made, to join the two others.

Arthur's sword-arm was caught helpless in the coils of Astaris' one tentacle. The other wrapped Louis' waist and held his kicking, flailing body too far from the Doctil to reach him with his dagger. Elijah, amazingly here, sprang with me in between the two, the prophet's gnarled hands clawed, my own fisted and flailing.

My fists never landed. Something caught my arms, pinned them. A dark tentacle squeezed my chest, numbing me. Had Astaris sprouted another? No. A Plebo held Elijah in a similar grip. I twisted my head and saw that it was a Plebo too who held me. Others came through the backwall of the niche, wrested away Arthur's sword, plucked the Dauphin's weapon from his fingers. Astaris released Arthur and the youngster to Plebos, who held them helpless.

A scream, shrill and terror-filled, cut through to me. Evelyn's scream! It gave me strength to drive legs into the floor, fighting madly to get loose. I staggered my captor, wrestled him around, but could not get free of him. The crowding, bulbous forms of the Doctil's bodyguard hid Eve from me. Her scream had choked off.

I tried to call to her, but a splayed hand was clamped over my mouth. I could see neither Astaris nor my companions in the attack on him. Around me were only the Plebos' great, goggling eyes, their tiny mouths, their pulsing head-membranes. The golden light was fading. The explosion of super-strength Evelyn's cry had aroused in me was gone. I slumped, nerveless with fear for her but emptied of strength and hope.

The crowd of Future Men seemed somehow thinner. I heard Arthur, below me. "Nay, there is no need to keep tight hold of me. I have yielded." I heard Evelyn. "Have they hurt you, Johnny?" All tenderness. "Johnny, have they hurt you?"

And I heard a reply. "No, dear. I'm all right." *My voice.* In timbre and accent, my voice. But I had not spoken!

I lifted my head, my brow wrinkling. The niche was black-dark now, but the blocking Plebos were gone and there was light enough out there in the vast vault that I could look out and down to its floor. The group down there was moving away. Guarded by three Plebos, I saw Elijah's majestic form, Arthur's. I saw Orth. The Dauphin. Evelyn.

Someone walked beside Evelyn, his arm thrown protectingly across her shoulders. Had Villon returned? No. The man was taller than the poet, more heavily built. He was dressed in a very modern brown suit. His hair was a reddish brown, and something about the poise of his head was familiar.

He turned as if to answer some remark of Evelyn's.

I made out very clearly, a semi-circular scar on his left cheek.

I made out his profile.

It was mine!

It was I who walked beside Evelyn, talked to her. It was I against whom she shrank, finding courage in the feet of my arm, strength in my nearness to meet whatever fate the Plebos marched her off to.

How could I be there, and here too?

"Evelyn!" I shouted. "That's not —" And checked, realizing that the Plebo's palm on my lips muffled my cry. I kicked backward, felt my heel crunch against the pipestem leg of my captor, lurched forward. Went over the niche edge, thudded on the floor below. A weight smothered me and something pounded the side of my head, pounded me down into a sick oblivion.

I lay on the bosom of a shoreless, turgid tide that heaved beneath me. My throat was parched. My head seemed to have ballooned to quadruple its normal size. This was the granddaddy of all hangovers, all right. I couldn't remember where I'd accumulated it, though I recalled very vividly the nightmare I'd just been riding, with its weird mess of Future Men and men out of the past; I recalled something about a terrible doom that overhung the world. Evelyn Rand had been in the dream, of course. I'd found her and had fallen in love with her and she with me, but the dream had wound up with me watching myself walk away from myself, having stolen my girl from me.

Well, I'd better get up and fix myself a Prairie Oyster and try to get into shape. Old Persimmon Puss Conklin will give me the fish eyes if I come strolling into the office late, and the Head will be sure to hear that I displayed every evidence of having had a hard night out.

Without trying to unglue my eyelids, I shoved myself up, groaning. Gingerly balancing on my aching shoulders that grossly enlarged head of mine, I wiggled a leg sidewise to get it down off the edge of the bed.

It wouldn't go down. The devil! Was I paralyzed? No liquor ever hit me this hard before. Wonder who brought me home. Or am I home? Bed feels awful damned hard. Better get eyes open and look around.

I went to work on the left one first. It slit, widened. And then the right flew open, and I was jumping to my feet.

I hadn't been able to get my leg down because it was already down. The bed was so hard because it was the stone floor of a small, cell-like chamber whose walls, polished, blue-gray rock, had neither window nor door, nor opening of any kind. I looked up. The blue-gray ceiling was solid as the walls.

It was no nightmare I'd been living. It was stark, incredible reality. I was a prisoner of the Doctils, in the Land where Time is Not, and Evelyn —

Was Evelyn already out on the plain, prey to the *drina!* Why she and not me? Why had she and the others been taken off, and I left behind? It was I who'd led the fight against the Doctils, I who had engaged in an unequal battle of wits with them. Why should I be spared-? Wait. Hadn't I seen myself being marched off with the others, brown suit, scarred cheek —

Hold everything! That had not been I out on the black floor. It couldn't have been. Even the Doctils, with all their million years advantage over the science I knew, couldn't make two of me, each complete.

I stood rigid in the center of that cell, trembling a little as I tried to recall every detail of what had occurred. There had been our attack on Astaris, the incursion of the Plebos to frustrate it. Fighting uselessly with the one who'd seized me, I'd lost sight of my companions, of Astaris. When that futile fight was over, I'd glimpsed the men of my own time again, and Evelyn. But — I was certain of it now — nowhere had I seen Astaris.

While that fight was going on, the girl had been hidden from me by the crowding Plebos. By the same token, I must have been hidden from her. I still had been hidden from her when it was over, but she spoke to me.

I could almost hear her now, "Johnny, are you hurt?"

It wasn't of me she had asked that, then, but of my double. And it was my double who had replied, in a perfect imitation of my voice. "No, dear. I'm all right." King Arthur had already been taken down out of the niche, and so probably had the others. I should have been taken down out of it too, unless there was a definite reason why I should not.

Was it by accident that the Plebos had crowded around me, hiding me from my friends? Hiding me from Evelyn? Very little the Future Men did was accidental.

I recalled how Astaris had projected Evelyn's presence, her personality, before me in that Brooklyn house. I recalled how, in a twinkling, Daster had taken on the exact appearance, the mannerisms, of a professor of my own time.

If I were building up a case in court, I could have established no better one to confirm the startling hypothesis I had not yet dared to put into words. Opportunity: A brawling fight in which I'd been concealed from view. Ability: Demonstrated.

My double was Astaris! Achronos Astaris had assumed my shape, my voice. He had become me!

Motive? The caress in his tones, his arm tender across Eve's shoulder, betrayed that. By spying, by threats, by persuasion, the

Doctil had failed to wring from Evelyn and me the secret of the love that lay between us, but he had not given up. He was trying another method now. Somewhere, in his wandering through the ages, he had become aware of the fact that love often begets love. He knew that Evelyn loved me. By becoming me he would become the object of her love and perhaps it would arouse that emotion in him so that he could study it by introspection.

"Damn him!" I cursed aloud. "Oh damn him!" shaken by a white and blistering rage, a jealous fury that blazed through my veins. And then I realized that I should be grateful, instead, that the Doctil had evolved this scheme.

As long as he still thought that it might work, Evelyn was safe. It was a greater protection for her than any I could give her.

What protection could I give her, what help could I be to her, against the Future Men? Physically, I was no match for them. Mentally, they had outmaneuvered my every attempt to match wits with them. But there was no shame in that. Not Einstein, not Michelson or Compton, not all of the outstanding intellects of my world and my age would make a better showing, pitted against them.

That might happen too. *That would happen.* It was only a matter of time. When they were ready —

The full and terrible implication of their plans, its promise of disaster to the civilization out of which I'd been plucked, swept down on me like a tangible black pall. I had flung defiance at them, but that defiance had been meaningless as the snarl of a week-old kitten at a Great Dane.

I stared at the seamless stone wall of my prison, stared at visions of New York's sky-reaching towers shattering down on terror-ridden crowds that fled to safety where there was no safety, of humans shrivelling in the blast of rays seething out of a menacing sky, of a civilization gone mad with the mad sound that filled the air, of flame-eyed men killing, killing one another, their arms, their clawed hands, dripping with gore.

And when the cataclysm was ended, I imagined the pitiful, mindless remnants of my race enslaved to the creatures of the Future who claimed to be men — "John!" A voice penetrated these appalling mental pictures. "It is you, my old. It is verily you!"

His velvet doublet more ragged than ever, the lace at his wrists and his throat more dingy, but with the same jaunty swagger to his meagre form, the same mocking smile on his thin, scar-twisted lips, Francois Villon stood beside me!

"Francois!" I gasped. "Where — how did you get in here? Where have you been? How-?"

"Softly!" Villon had laid a long finger beside his hawklike nose. "Softly, my cabbage. If you will permit me to answer one query before you prod me with another — I entered this cell in the same manner you were brought here, through its wall."

"Through-! Then there's a secret door —"

"My liver, John, no! They are solid of stone, all four walls, floor and ceiling. It is through the solid stone I came, as they do, by help of this." There was, in the hand he held out to me, a tiny mechanism of what seemed like platinum wiring and glass or fused quartz. "The Doctils need little beside the power of their brains to perform their magic, but the Plebos are of lesser mould. They require this — key, shall we name it for want of a better term — to translate themselves through matter without door or aperture. It is of a Plebo I had it, the one I saw carrying you off, when I returned to join you in the Hall of Miracles. He did not hear me follow him, nor will he miss what I have taken from him." He touched, delicately, the hilt of his poniard, and I saw at the throat of its scabbard an edging of red, sticky wet that had wiped from the blade as it slid into its tight sheath.

"The poet," Villon smiled slyly, "is also a master thief."

And a Paris apache, I thought, recalling what I had read of this strangest character in all literature. "Where did they take Evelyn and the others?" I asked him, trying not to repress a shudder at the way he could blandly smile, after what he had done.

"Nay, that I do not know. They were out of sight. Perhaps, if I had returned a moment sooner —" he shrugged his bony shoulders.

"Returned from where? When I saw you were gone I thought they had taken you —"

"They did not take me. I went of my own accord, and they did not know it. I —"

"They did not know! But they can read our thoughts. How-?"

"Name of a dog, but you make one imbecile with your questions! They read our thoughts only when they bend their own upon ours. To show us the scenes they cast upon the screen of the wall, to bring us into them as part of them, demanded all of their minds, to watch them took all the minds of you others. But me, I shut out from mine that shadow-play and watched the Doctils themselves, hoping that in an unguarded moment I might see something that might be of aid to us."

"And you did?"

He shrugged again, and though he still smiled, I thought there was a shimmer of fear in his eyes. "I saw something, but whether it gives us hope or is the death of all hope for us, I do not yet know. A long space of time I saw only five shapes in a high niche from which the golden light had faded, five monstrous shapes wholly intent on seizing our senses to make them toys of their wills. Fighting that intent, I sweated like a whipped coach horse. Then there was a stir among them. The strain upon me loosened, and meseemed some distracting word had come to them. I recall that there was a stir among you others also, as though their grip upon you had grown less strong."

"We came to ourselves," I interrupted, "for a moment or so. I wonder if it was then."

"Aye," Villon nodded. "It may well have been, for methought I heard Elijah cry out something about denying God. But four of the five Doctils were hastening away, and I did not turn for I was skulking after them and feared to lose sight of the four in the dimness."

Four. One had remained behind. It had taken the whole Kintat to hypnotize us so that we seemed to relive the whole evolution of civilization and its destruction, but once we were under the influence, Astaris had been able to hold us alone.

"They went out of that Hall of Midnight," Villon continued, "and out of the House of Sun. Me, I dared not emerge to the open, for fear that I might be spied."

"You stopped!" I exclaimed. "You let them get away from you!"

"Name of the name of a dog, will you let me tell my tale? What I saw, I saw, and if you have no wish to learn what that was, I am content to make silent."

"I'm sorry, Villon," I apologized. "I'll keep still. What did you see?"

"Nothing, at first, for that a white glare filled the Bowl of Adalon, and it blinded my eyes that were used to the dimness. There was a vast hissing in the sky, like a thousand flying serpents giving vent to their hate of our captors. I peered on high, striving to make out whence came that monstrous reptilian sound.

"The white light streamed from the top of the tower we saw building, that top ablaze as though it had impaled the Sun. The glare roofed the pit, from rampart to rampart of the cliffs that form it. It was only stray beams from it that dazzled me below, up there it was a very white hell of light in which nothing could live.

"Adown the walls of the bowl dribbled streamlets, graypurple and slow, as though at the brink of the cliffs the light from the tower melted something like fire melts wax. And this indeed was the case, as I descried when my aching sight became more accustomed to the glare.

"Circling the verge of the Bowl a dark cloud lay against the Veil of Ishlak, a heaving cloud that was not a cloud at all but thousands upon thousands of the weird creatures that people the plains where we found each other, you and I. The drina. The Veil, or so it seemed to me, was a little rent here and there, and where it was rent the gray-purple flesh of the drina oozed through, striving to rend the Veil still further, and there that flesh was melting in the white blaze from the tower and running in slow streamlets down the cliffs."

"I thought the Veil was impenetrable," I could not keep from again breaking into Villon's narrative, "unless the Future Men opened it themselves from some control down here."

"So it is," Francois agreed. "The drina masses boiled, behind each opening in it, about a stratcar, its shining plates torn apart, its shining form crushed. The Veil had been opened in each of those places to let a stratcar through, and some of the drina had blocked its closing again, were writhing through while their fellows swamped the flying machines that had been sent to hold them off while the tower was being completed. The drina were writhing through, and the blaze from the tower, now completed, was melting them as fast as they oozed through, and still they came in an implacable dark tide of hate."

"God," I whispered, "they're brave. No human army —"

"Not brave," Villon denied, "but mad. The drina know no fear, my John, because they are without minds to know fear. They are animate only with hate and the lust to kill. Now indeed such an enemy is the worst of all, for only by destruction can they be defeated, only by complete and utter obliteration. Against thinking beings like us, against all the armies our world could muster against them, the Future Men would be invincible. Seeing that our weapons were powerless against them, seeing that our defences were powerless against theirs, panic would turn our blood to water, our strength to weakness, and we would be undone. But these imbecile monsters that attack them —"

"Haven't sense enough to know when they're licked. By all that's holy, Francois, the Doctils may have beaten themselves." I was recalling how they'd deliberately destroyed the minds of this planet's natives, had deliberately made them the idiot things they were. "But go on. Is that battle still on?"

"Yes — and no. The Veil is whole again, and no drina has achieved the Bowl. The Plebos, it seems, were able only to obey instructions. They had been directed to delay the gray-purple hosts with the stratcars till the tower was finished and then to destroy them with the white light from the tower. This they did, but when the combat raged too evenly for comfort, they summoned the Kintat. With the advent of the Doctils a new phase of the fight set in. I saw a great scurrying about. I saw Plebos swarm up the tower bearing new devices. And then the light that seethed from it was no longer white. Crackling streamers of blue and scarlet and eye-searing yellow flashed overhead, seeking the rents in the Veil. The flesh of the attackers no longer melted but whiffed into nothingness. The breaches in the shimmering barrier were repaired, and the blaze at the tower-top sputtered out."

The excitement that had made me forget my despair drained out of me, "Then the Doctils have won. Why did you let me think-?"

"They have not altogether conquered, my friend. The Veil of Ishlak is whole again, and in the Bowl they are safe, but against the Veil still billows the gray-purple mass of the drina, and beyond the Veil the Future Men dare not venture. They are prisoners in Adalon, our captors, til they devise some means to destroy their besiegers."

"We mustn't let them do that." My fingers dug into the poet's scrawny arm. "We've got to find a way to keep them from doing that, Villon. We've got to find a way to let the drina get through the Veil and come down into the Bowl —"

"John!" He pulled back from me, his widened eyes on mine. "Have you gone mad? Do you not realize that if the drina gain Adalon we too, all of us, will die with the Plebos and the Doctils? Those loathsome masses will roll over us, my friend, and we will be taken up within them, and their acids will rot us —"

"Let them. So long as the Future Men are wiped out, let the drina wipe us out too. All of us."

"All, John?" Francois' gaze probed my brain. "Even Evelyn, John?"

An icy shudder ran through me. "Even Evelyn, Francois, if I cannot kill her with my own hand before that happens. If she were here, she would tell you the same."

"No," the poet sighed. "There is no madness in your eves. But why, then-?"

I told him. I told him, briefly, what we had seen, and what we had learned the Kintat planned. "You agree with me, Francois?" I asked when I had finished. "You agree with me that they must be wiped out, even if we have to be wiped out with them?"

There was no smile on his lips, and his countenance was gray under its blue stubble. "Aye, John," he answered. "No matter how terrible a death it be, our death in the bowels of the drina would be a cheap price to pay for the destruction of these demons."

CHAPTER 22

THE DEATH CLOUD

"CHEAP ENOUGH," I LAUGHED CURTLY.

"I'd set the value of our lives right now, at two dozen for a nickle, and that's too high if we hang around in here much longer. You say that thing you've got there is a key to this cell. If it is, let's go. Let's get out of here . . . What's the matter?"

Villon was looking at the involved device in his palm, and something like dismay was in his face.

"It is a key," he said slowly. "And yet it is no key. It passed me, singly, in through the stone but — will it take two of us out?"

"The only way to find out is to try. Look. When we left the stratcar hangar through its wall, Daster had his hand on my back. When the plain rushed past us as we came to Adalon, Kass had his hands on the two of us. Maybe I ought to be touching you while you try to use that."

"Of a surety you must touch me." Francois' smile was wan. "Thus, if the magic of this thing avails to carry us into the stone but not through it, we shall at least be immured with a comrade near to accompany us into oblivion."

That was what he was afraid of. That the power of the 'key' might be enough to get us into the rock, yet not sufficient to take both of us all the way through it. I admit the thought was not exactly pleasant.

"Well," I put my arm around his narrow shoulders, "It will be an interesting experiment." I could feet the shudder that was running through him. "Come on." I'd hate to be cursed with your imagination, I thought, aware that he was picturing himself caught within the rock, entombed there forever . . .

I have a pretty good imagination too.

"Come on, old man," I urged. "Let's get it over with," and pressed him toward the wall through which he'd come.

A muscle twitched in his sallow cheek. He lifted his hand, placed the 'key' against the bluish, perdurable rock. "It was done thus," he murmured, "as I watched. And then, the Plebo pressed — this." His thumb moved.

There was no change in the appearance of the wall. "Damn!" I muttered. "It doesn't work." I struck the stone with my free hand — and my fist went into it! I stepped forward, pressed Villon with me.

The world blanked out. I felt nothing, saw nothing but featureless grayness. I seemed to be still moving forward, but the grayness pressed in on me, held me. I gasped voicelessly. Then, after one fearful instant, the grayness was gone, and I was in a dim corridor and Francois was beside me. The floor of the hall pitched steeply down, curving to the left, ran steeply up, curving to the right, but just here it was level.

Neither of us said anything for a long minute. Neither of us could have said anything if our lives depended on it.

Then, "It's done," I heard Villon say, and he was jaunty again when I turned to him, his black eyes sparkling with triumph. "We are through."

"Yes," I agreed, "we're through." I wasn't as happy over that as I might have been. I had spied an unmoving form sprawled at our feet and the skin on my back was crawling. Alive, a Plebo is not a pretty sight. Dead — imagine a dead spider big as a man, all eyes, all glazed, fishy eyes . . .

Villon was looking at it too. "He died easily," he murmured, "for so ungainly a creature."

"I don't like leaving him here." I tried to imitate my companion's nonchalance. "Anyone coming along this passage will at once know something's gone wrong, and it may mean the loss of precious minutes for us. I wish there was somewhere we could hide him."

"There is," Francois responded. "Right at hand."

"Where?" I glanced around, puzzled, saw nothing but bare walls.

"In here." The poet laid his palm against the wall we'd just penetrated. "If they do not find him till they come for you, we shall have lost none of those jewelled minutes of which you speak."

There was no argument as to that, but could it be done? "I suppose one of us might carry the corpse in," I ventured. "But, I'd rather not take the chance of your 'key' failing to work."

"Nor I," Villon shrugged. "But perhaps our friend need not be carried in there. There is strength in those rounded muscles of yours, my old, and I suspect that whether he goes all the way through or not will not matter to him."

I got his idea. "All right. We'll try it." I bent and lifted the dead Plebo while Francois placed the 'key' against the wall. The cadaver was lighter than I'd expected. Dangling from my grasp, it seemed almost boneless. "Ready?"

Villon's thumb pressed, and I threw the corpse at the wall. Threw it *through* the wall. It went into the blue, solid-seeming stone as though that stone were merely an opaque fog.

There was no evidence left of the Plebo, out here in the corridor, except a small, dark stain on its floor.

"I should like to be there," Francois chuckled, "when they discover him in that cell, and you gone. Will they think, I wonder, that we are masters of a magic they do not know?"

"They'll know damned well what's happened, and they'll be after us like a shot. The only reason I can figure out for their not having missed you yet is that they're so busy with strengthening their defences against the drina. If we're to accomplish anything we've got to get going."

"You have right," he agreed. "Which way shall we be going, up or down?"

I wanted to say down. That way would lead out of the House of Sun, would lead to the House of Earth. They must have taken the others there, back to the room where humans from all the centuries awaited the dreaded summons. They must have taken Evelyn there, and Astaris, posing as me. My blood was hot again with anger and the thought of the Doctil receiving the tenderness intended for me hammered at my skull. I understood how a man could kill and have no compunction at killing.

"Which way, my old?" Villon asked again.

"Up!" I answered. "When the Veil opened to let through the stratcar which Kass summoned, I noticed a flash near the top of this building. The control for the Veil must be somewhere above, and if we can get to that —"

"We may be able to raise the Veil and let the drina down into the Bowl!" Villon finished for me. "You are right; up it is."

And so we climbed upward along the steep spiral of that passage, while with me went the thought of Evelyn and Astaris and what might be, what must be, passing between them. It doesn't matter, I tried to tell myself. It doesn't matter at all. Before she discovers that the man to whose caresses she gives herself is not the Johnny she has loved since childhood, he will be dead, and she will be dead, and the only living things left in the Bowl of Adalon will be the mindless creatures they call the drina.

We seemed to have been climbing eternally, the curving of the passage hiding what was behind us, and what was ahead. "Like the living of life this is," Villon murmured. "A blind and toilsome mounting whose aim we do not know. And when the end is attained, we find it to be — nothing."

"There's something at the top of this climb," I growled. "There's got to be."

The spiral levelled out for a distance of about ten feet. Ahead it started climbing again — Villon's clutch on my arm brought me to a halt. "Hearken," he whispered, his long, grimy forefinger stabbing toward the slope.

I heard what he meant. A faint whisper of movement, far ahead, far above. Vague sounds brought to us by the resonance of the tunnel.

"Some of them are up there," I murmured. "In the passage, and coming this way. We've got to go back before they spy us."

"We'll not go back," Francois murmured, low-toned. "Hearken once more, my poor friend."

There were faint sounds behind us now, behind and below. Our retreat was cut off.

The poet's laugh was soundless, but in his eyes there were the same bitterness and the same despair as had been in the laugh with which he'd greeted the appearance of Kass. "They play with us, my old," he whispered. "They play with us as a cat with a mouse, or as a certain jailer of Paris with his prisoners, permitting that they escape from their dungeon only to attain, after much travail, another more foul and noisome." His poniard slid from its sheath. "But they shall not take me, alive." The dagger, stained with the blood of the Plebo he'd killed, flashed to his breast —

I caught his wrist before the point had more than pricked the velvet. "No, you fool," I grunted. "We're not caught yet. The passage is level here, like it was outside my cell. That may mean we're at another story of the building and that behind one of these walls there's a chamber in which we can hide."

"It may. It well may." His eyes were sparkling again. "And those we hear coming may be proceeding on their own affairs, not hunting us. But behind which wall, my old, lies safety?"

"Nothing like finding out. This side's my guess. It's this side the cell was on. Where's that 'key'? Quick. They're a lot nearer."

I grabbed Villon's arm and his hand went up to the wall I'd indicated. I was going through the grayness again, but I was getting quite used to that. What bothered me was whether there was a room on the other side of the wall, or whether it had become the outside wall of the building so that, once through, we'd go hurtling down —

We didn't. We came out smoothly, safely, on the other side — I crouched, forcing Francois down with me, my pulses pounding.

The space into which we had come was low-ceiled but long and wide. It was bare as the cell from which Villon had rescued me, but it was occupied.

At one end King Arthur and Orth and Louis were seated on the floor, Elijah erect not far from them. Nearer us Evelyn Rand walked leisurely about.

And strolling beside her *was — myself!*

"Magic!" Villon gasped. "John is here and he is there, and —" My palm over his mouth muffled the rest. Too late. Astaris had turned, was looking straight at us with my eyes, out of my face. But he did not see us. He could not have seen us, for that turn of his had been slow and leisurely and Evelyn had turned with him. She had not seen us either for now they were walking slowly away, hand in hand as a couple of lovers might walk beneath a silver moon.

"Johnny," I heard Evelyn murmur. "Are you sure it wasn't all something we dreamed? What we've gone through can't be real, and this too. This garden, this quiet peace, and you here with me, it's all just as I pictured it, longingly, all those lonely years."

"Why worry," I heard my own low voice answer from the lips of that other who was so like me I might be looking in a mirror. "This is real for now, this loveliness. Don't think of anything else. Think of me. Think of how much you love me, and of how —" He hesitated.

"Yes, Johnny?"

"And of how I love you." He was looking down at her now, with a curious eagerness. "Tell me, my very dear, how I love you, and why."

They were only a pace from us now, and yet there was no hint that either was aware of our presence. I felt Villon quiver, under my restraining hand.

"Why don't you *tell* me, Johnny?" They angled, as though turning the corner of a path where I could see only naked floor. "A girl wants to hear things like that from her lover." They were walking parallel to the wall against which we crouched, about a yard from it.

"Does she? I wouldn't know, Eve. I don't know how a lover should speak and act. Will you teach me?"

"Doesn't your own heart teach you-? Oh look!" She stopped, half turning to the wall. "Isn't this forsythia lovely?" Her slim hand reached out to empty air, but her fingers seemed to be touching something that wasn't there. "It's just like the bush near the gate of our fence where I waited for you, years ago."

I got it! Jumping Jupiter, I got it! Eve saw a garden, shrubbery, where there was nothing at all but gray rock. The others — I threw a swift glance at them and saw Orth's fingers trail along the floor as one trails his fingers through sod, saw Louis gesture as though he picked up a twig and threw it from him — were victims of the same illusion. It was just one more instance of the mass hypnotism, the capture of our weaker minds by those infinitely more powerful, tremendously better trained, that I had already experienced more than once. Its purpose, this time, was clear.

Astaris had arranged a romantic setting for his laboratory experiment in romance.

Villon and I were not affected by the illusion because the Doctil did not know of our presence. And this implied that he also saw this bare space as, a lovely garden, that to him also there appeared to be shrubbery here where we crouched, forsythia bushes that concealed us.

Could this be because he was himself the real subject of the experiment and so deliberately was exposing himself to its conditions, or because, assuming my eyes, my brain, he had also assumed my susceptibility to the mass hypnosis? It didn't matter. What mattered was that we were hidden from him by those illusory bushes.

"Don't move," I muttered in Francois' ear. "Don't make a sound." And then I was stealing away from him, crouched low, was creeping stealthily toward Evelyn and her companion, their backs still toward me.

I had to guess how far the invisible shrubbery extended. I had to take the chance that my very real body would not rustle those unreal leaves. All I could do was to make no sound on the corporeal rock across which I stole.

I got within a yard of the two and sprang. My fist flailed, pounded the jointure of spine and brain-case where a blow is certain to stun a man. My victim thudded soggily to the floor.

Evelyn whirled, screaming. Her scream cut off, and only a gasp came from her throat. There was no color in her face, her lips. Her pupils were dilated.

A strangled shout came from behind me. "The garden — where?" There was the trample of feet running toward us. There was Arthur's bellow, "Ho, varlet —"

"Evelyn!" My arms went out to her, my hands found her shoulders. "Eve! Don't look at me like that. I'm real. I'm your Johnny. He wasn't —" Fingers bruised my own shoulder, twisted me around. I saw Orth's furious countenance, King Arthur's.

"John!" the latter exclaimed. "John March. Thou art he indeed. But then who-?"

"Astaris," I told him. "One of the Doctils. He took my shape. He made you think he was I."

The king pulled the edge of his hand across his eyes, his face ghastly. "Magicked again. A moment ago we were stretched on greensward, besides a purling stream. Now — these walls, this footing and ceil of bare stone —"

"Wait." It was Orth who had grabbed me, and he had not let me go. "How do we know this one is March and not —" He cut off. He was gaping down at the floor and a green pallor spread across his blunt jawed countenance. "Ach Gott!"

I twisted as far as his hold on me would permit, looked to see what had affected him so. It wasn't my double that lay unconscious at

Evelyn's feet. It was Achronos Astaris in his proper shape; tentacular limbs, bulbous small body clothed in its orange integument, enormous head, all complete. The huge eyes were sightless, staring.

"Now you know which one of us is the real John March," I grated, jerking free from the Archduke's clutch. "Get him tied up, with your belts, with everything you've got that can be made into ropes, before he comes to."

"He must not be permitted to come to, John," Villon's quiet voice said. "Tie him as we may, we cannot prevent him from sending a mental message to his fellows." The poet dropped to his knees beside Astaris, and his poniard was in his fingers.

"No!" I cried. "No, Francois!" He looked up at me, his shaggy brows quizzical, his twisted smile mocking. "Oh, I haven't any feeling for him, but we thought Arthur's idea of holding him as a hostage was a good one, and it still may be. We'll tie him up, and we'll keep him stunned. We'll watch him every minute, and the instant he shows signs of regaining consciousness, we'll conk him again."

"He is right, Villon," Orth supported me. "It may do us some good or not, but to keep him alive yet awhile cannot do harm."

The Frenchman shrugged. "Perhaps. Yet I would fear him less if he were dead."

"We approve of our John's advice," Arthur put an end to the discussion. "The creature shall be bound, and we, in our own proper person, shall make it our charge that he remains asleep."

I left the others to tie up the Doctil, got to the girl's side. "Eve!" She was rigid, her tiny face still and pallid.

"What's wrong?" My arm was around her, I was drawing her close to me.

Her mouth twisted. "I — I kissed him, Johnny. I gave my kiss to that — Thing."

"It was I you gave that kiss to, darling," I murmured. "You thought it was I you were giving it to, and that makes it all right. Or it will, as soon as you correct the misdelivery."

"Will it, Johnny?" That tight mouth of hers broke into a tremulous smile. "Will it?"

It seemed to. At any rate the tenseness went out of her, and she was very sweet, very warm, in my arms.

We were reminded that we were not alone in some ecstatic solitude by Louis' boyishly plaintive voice. "I wish someone would tell me where the garden went to. I liked it. It was the first time I'd viewed grass and flowers since I was a very little boy."

"Oh, you poor kid," Evelyn exclaimed. Pulling free of me, she ran to him, put her arm around him. "You poor, poor child. They put you in prison when you were only nine years old, didn't they?"

"The garden wasn't real, Louis," I told him. "Astaris made you all 'see' it, and when I knocked him out he couldn't make you see it any longer."

"There will be no gardens anywhere, John," Villon drawled, "if we spend our time on kisses and prattle. Have you forgotten the mission on which we set out?"

"What mission?" Orth demanded. I told them about the *drina's* attack, about our plan to attempt to lift the Veil of Ishlak and let them into the Bowl. "There is no doubt in my mind that if the creatures are powerful enough to keep the Veil from closing, they will be able to tear down every building in Adalon," I ended. "And so there will be no safety from them for anyone in Adalon, for Plebos or Doctils — or us. Villon and I made the decision for you, my friends, when you were not there to ask, because we felt that is how you would want it. Were we right?"

Elijah was the first to answer me. "Gladly would I embrace the Angel of Death, knew I that in the same dark flight he would bear off those heathen who have denied their Creator and would destroy His work." Looking about at the faces of the others, I read confirmation in their grave lineaments, their level gaze. I sought Evelyn's.

"I could not love you," she said, simply, "if I thought you would consider saving my life at the cost of letting them carry out their dreadful plan. I am not afraid to die, Johnny, now that I have been in your arms."

"All right," I said, crisply to hide the emotion that was tearing at my throat. "We'll go ahead with it then, if we can. But I'd give a lot to know what's going on out there. If they've already driven the drina away, or destroyed them, there would be no use in our trying to find the place from which the Veil is controlled. But as it's impossible for us to find that out, I —"

"*Monsieur* Marsh!" Louis interrupted. "I think that perhaps you can do that. When first we were left alone in this garden I saw you — this Doctil who pretended to be you — gazing into something that appeared like a mirror, thinking himself unobserved. I wondered then what he saw in it that made him look afraid and angry, both at once. Maybe this thing he looked into was no mirror at all, but —"

"Some device similar to television," I finished for him. "In taking my form he seems to have lost a great many of his mental powers, and he'd want to keep in touch-. If we can find it —" I turned to Astaris' bound form, and saw that Villon was already kneeling to it, his long, deft fingers searching it.

"This that he wears is skin-tight as the costumes of the tumblers who amuse the rabble on Seine's bank of a feastday," the poet reported. "It gives no space for the concealment — Ah!" he broke off. His hand came out from under the body it was searching, and there was a gleaming plate in it, circular and about the size of a woman's hand glass. "It lay beneath him. Your clothing, on him, was an illusion, but this is real."

"I hope the fall hasn't put it out of commission." I reached for it. "Let me see." He gave it to me.

The thing looked very much like the toilet article to which I've compared it, except that it had no handle. It was somewhat thicker too, and the edge of the disk was serried with tiny protuberances. The mirror itself was oddly milky, so that in it the reflections, of my face and of Evelyn and the others crowding about me to peer into it, were vague and wraithlike.

"Post thou see aught?" King Arthur demanded, glanced at him. He was watching the recumbent Doctil, his scabbarded sword held clublike in his big hands. He wasn't allowing curiosity to distract him from his self-delegated task of keeping our hostage unconscious and innocuous. "What dost thou see?"

"Nothing," I answered, my voice flat with disappointment. "It's a washout."

"Johnny!" Eve exclaimed. "Those bumps on the edge look like push-buttons. Why don't you try pressing them?"

"Good girl!" The excrescences were indeed movable. I squeezed them.

The misty reflections vanished from the glass. It was clear, abruptly, and glowing. But it showed only a meaningless jumble; broken shapes of stone, corners, canted walls, a disjointed tentacle, a single great eye, the confused pieces of a jig-saw puzzle or a surrealist's nightmare. "Damn!" I grunted. "It's television all right. But I can't make head or tail —"

"He held it like this." The Dauphin grabbed the rim of the disk, tugged at it till I was holding it vertically. The chaos slid beneath its surface as it moved, and changed kaleidoscopically, but it was still a chaos.

"Oh," Eve stamped her foot. "It's exasperating."

"Wait!" I grunted. "I'm like a kid with a toy piano, banging all the keys at once." I let all save one of the buttons come up. "That does it!"

Etched crystal-clear in the mirror was the corridor where Villon and I almost had been caught. "The buttons control the distance the thing sees, and by pressing all of them I was superimposing layer after layer of this building upon one another, like a dozen transparent pictures." A Plebo went by in the glass descending, some peculiarly shaped instrument in his hand. Another followed him. "They're still looking for Francois and me."

"I doubt that," Orth disputed me. "These people better ways of finding you will have than running around like chickens with the heads chopped off. For example, they must have more than one of these glasses and with them in minutes they could scan the whole of Adalon."

"He has right, John," Francois agreed. "Me, I think they hasten to the defence of their city. Perchance the drina once more have pierced the Veil."

"We'll soon see. Which way was Astaris facing this when you saw him use it, Louis?"

The youngster showed me, and then, as I pressed buttons in rotation, room after room of the House of Sun appeared in the mirror and flicked off. I should have liked to examine each but it was more important to determine what the situation was outside.

The last button brought a vista of the Bowl of Adalon into the round glass.

The aspect of its level floor had not changed much from when we'd crossed it, shepherded by Daster, except that the girders no longer flowed across it to the tower, and that the tower was finished. A number of Plebos were clustered around its base and Favril and Bolar were among them, but it was up the lacy spire that my eyes lifted — to where its apex, level with the rim of the bowl, was surmounted by a wide platform that held a knot of Plebos and Daster and several machines whose nature I could not make out.

The occupants of the platform were looking outward and there was something in their posture that told me that they were afraid. I canted the small glass to bring what they gazed at into its circle, and I saw.

I saw the brink of the cliff and the grayish purple cloud that mounded monstrously there, more menacing than any thunderhead. It was not storm with which that cloud was pregnant but hate and the lust to kill and the vilest of deaths. It was not cloud. It was a massing of a myriad pulsing bodies merged by their own weight, their own avid pressure into one, and it was restrained only by the shimmer of force Villon had called the Veil of Ishlak from pouring down upon Adalon.

And in Adalon the men of the future watched the dark and mindless death brooding over their city and were afraid. If the veil should yield to its awful thrust they would perish horribly — and we with them.

But Earth, the Earth of the Twentieth Century, would be saved.

Somehow I must find a way to make the Veil yield.

As these thoughts flashed through my mind, John Orth groaned. "Mother of all Living. This is horror —"

"That's it!" I exclaimed. "That may be the answer." An idea that may have lain beneath the surface of my mind all this time had broken through. "Maybe," I said trembling with sudden hope, "maybe we don't have to die after all, my friends. Maybe we can save Earth from the Doctils without that."

CHAPTER 23

THE MOTHER OF ALL LIVING

"WHAT? — How? — JOHNNY, WHAT DO you mean?..." A tumult of questions beat at me, but I paid them no attention as I feverishly thumbed the button of the television disk that I'd first pressed, at the same time moving the device to focus again the corridor just outside this chamber.

The plan that had sprung into my mind was breathtaking in its simplicity, but there were many things I had to know before I could even attempt carrying it out. The level part of the passage was now empty of life. I moved the disk so as to follow the descending spiral and catch up with the last of the hurrying Plebos I'd glimpsed. The thing he carried was, in the same manner that a revolver is a miniature cannon, a miniature of one of the machines on the towertop.

"Yes," I muttered, "that must be it. They've been called together to guard something or someone tremendously important. Pray, Elijah. If you have any influence with your God, pray that it's in this building."

"Look here, March," Orth insisted. "We've got a right to know what you're up to." The Plebo I watched reached another of the level places in the ramp, halted, and turned to the blank wall. "What are you looking for?"

"You named it yourself, Orth. You handed it to me on a silver platter."

"I named it!" The Plebo melted into the wall and I manipulated buttons to follow him. "What did I name, John Marsh?"

The room that came into the disk was walled with silver and it was as large as the one we were in. Ten Plebos, each armed with a weapon such as the newcomer carried, stood in a circle and at its center on a raised dais the Doctil Gohret stood above a case of some transparent substance within which, couched on billows of white, softly gleaming silk lay — "Marsh!" Orth was insisting. "What was it I named?"

"The Mother of All Living," I answered him softly. "Look at her. The mother-to-be of all the living whom the Doctils intend shall inherit our own good green Earth when they have conquered it."

Within that case she was larger by far than any woman any of us have ever known, but she was formed like the women we knew and not like the grotesque beings of the Future who guarded her. Her skin was as white as the cushioned silk on which she lay nude, her eyes closed, and more lustrous. She was great-bosomed, huge-limbed, immensely wide of hip. Her face was possessed of pale, almost unearthly beauty but it was a bovine beauty, a mindless calm that made of her something less than human.

"The Matra," I breathed. "The Queen Bee. The spawner of ova for the Doctils and the only one of her kind left alive. From her they must get the seed of the superhumans of whom they dream, and without her their dream cannot be fulfilled. Without her they will be five Doctils and a hundred Plebos, and never any more. Without her there would be no point in their depopulating Earth of our race and our generation, for without her they could never repeople it again with theirs.

"That is why they guard her, and Gohret. If only one Doctil is left alive with her, he can recreate his race. If all of them escape the drina, but she dies, they are beaten."

"And so," Villon was the first to comprehend, "we must slay her."

"No, Johnny!" There was horror in Eve's cry. "She is a woman, a mother. It would be an unspeakable crime."

I twisted to her. "A crime, Eve, and unspeakable — but not mine. They are guilty of it who degraded womanhood to the level of a breeding machine. You call that Matra a mother, but is she? It takes love to make a mother, and years of fostering care. That poor creature will never know her offspring, never even see them. She is no more a mother than a hen whose eggs are taken from her as soon as they are laid and placed in an incubator to batch. And, Eve, million's upon millions of real mothers on the Earth of our time will die, as horribly as you saw the mothers of this planet die — if the Matra lives. If *she lives they* will die, and the children whom they have borne in suffering, and fed at their breasts, and agonised over, will die. It is the Matra's life against the lives of those mothers, one against millions."

I was justifying my proposal not only to her but to myself. It ran counter to all the tradition bred into me, to all I had been taught. I recalled with what horror I'd watched, in the twentieth century I was fighting to protect, bombs rain from the sky upon women, mothers —

"The Matra is not even a woman, Fraulein Evelyn," Orth put in. "Look how in that so beautiful face there is no hint of a soul, no semblance of thought. Were she a woman, did she know what she is and what is done with her, she would embrace death as a mercy and a blessed release."

"She — she is asleep," Evelyn objected, weakly. "Maybe if she were awake —"

"That isn't sleep, darling," I interrupted. "Look. That case is hermetically sealed. There is no way for air to get into it, let alone food.

She is in a state of suspended animation, a sort of living death. She is to all intents, already dead. It is only a very tiny spark of life that would be extinguished if she were killed."

The girl made a little, halting gesture with her hand. "You are right, Johnny, and I am wrong." And then she smiled tremulously and put her hand on my arm. "But look. If you can take her away from them and not kill her, they'd give anything to get her back. Promise me you won't kill her unless you have to. Please, Johnny, promise me that."

I would have promised her the world with a fence around it right then. "I promise, Eve."

The fluttering touch of her fingertips on my cheek was thanks enough.

"You promise much, John, and talk much about seizing the Matra or slaying her," Francois said softly. "But of how it is to be done you say nothing. Is it that you will enter that room, bow, and say prettily, 'Messieurs, I have come to slay her whom you guard, armed with weapons against which I have no means of attack. Pray stand while I slice her gullet.'"

He was right. I looked again into the disk, saw again the quiet, confident circle of Plebos around that gleaming casket, saw the orange-torsoed Gohret beside it, one splayed hand resting on its top. Of all the Kintat this one was the most implacable, the most nearly naked intelligence, the most formidable. What strength did we have, what strategy could we evolve, that could have any hope of success against him?

"Have faith in the Eternal, my son," Elijah intoned.

"The Most Holy arms the righteous with the lightnings of His wrath. Jehovah casts the cloak of His omnipotence about them who go forth to battle against His enemies."

"I fear me, sage," Villon's slurred accents took issue with him, "that your Jehovah has forsaken this land and all who people it. I seem to recall that its inhabitants were in the very act of worshipping Him, or Someone very like Him, when disaster fell upon them."

"Silence!" Arthur ordered. "We will not have this squabbling while our John March meditates upon the means to defeat the heathen."

And Louis was piping, "You'll win over them, *Monsieur* March. You will, I'm sure of it."

Whether I wished it or not, I had assumed the leadership of the little band. I had to justify their faith in me. I simply had to. "I'll work out some way of getting at the Matra," I told them, pretending a confidence I didn't feel. "But we ought to have two strings to our bow.

Suppose we see what chance there is of our carrying out our original idea, to lift the Veil of Ishlak and let the drina down into the Bowl."

I moved the disk, pressed the proper button. The scene outside flashed into the glass once more — the strange structures that were arranged as the planets of the Solar System are arranged, the defending tower with its cluster of Future Men about its base and on the platform at its top. Their tenseness, the slow throb of their ear-membranes, filled with a brooding fear the Bowl of Adalon.

The gray-purple mass of the drina pressed against the Veil, waiting. They'd wait there till the end of time if need be. Hate would keep them there, the hate that was the last remnant of mentality the conquerors of their world had left them. The lust to kill would keep them there, the blind lust to destroy that the maddening vibrations of those conquerors' sonic vibrators had instilled in them, a grisly exchange for the souls of which they had been robbed.

There seemed in this latter circumstance a twisted justice, a grotesque sort of retribution.

My throat tightened. One of those who crowded around me to look into the disk may have jolted my arm, or perhaps some obscure impulse had made me tip it a little, so that I was looking over the cloud of the drina and beyond it.

At any rate, silhouetted against the low brown sky, I saw something that had not been there before, that could not, I swear, before this have been seen from within the Bowl. Black, and so vast as to blot out a full quadrant of the sky in which it hung, I saw the statue that was my first memory of the Land Where Time is Not. The haunched body, the soaring legs, the hooded, awful head of a Being that was neither man nor beast.

Or was it the statue? Immense as it was, it seemed to have a quality of life that the great monument had not possessed. Was this because it was a mirage? Or was it? Reason rejected the other hypothesis. And yet — and yet, the tremendous apparition was not quite the same as the monument that had so astounded me. Its hood seemed lifted a little. The eyes still hidden with that hood seemed to be gazing down on the hosts of the drina. And something in the poise of that vast head, in the very lines of that monstrous body, seemed to speak of pity, and sorrow, and also of a patience that was reaching its end.

The others saw it too, they must have seen it. For I heard Elijah's rolling, orotund tones, answering Villon. "Oh little man of little faith. The Eternal is infinite and all-present. Nor in the uttermost reaches of the Firmament, nor in the ultimate end of Time, is there limit to Him, nor let to His majesty. For His own inscrutable purpose He may permit His faithful to suffer, but never, in the end, does He forsake them."

And for once Francois Villon had no mocking reply at the tip of his tongue.

CHAPTER 24

THE MAGNIFICENT FOOLS

THE PRESENCE IN THE BROWN SKY faded and was gone. It must after all, I told myself, have been a mirage. But I was not quite able to rid myself of a certain awe. I had seen Something few men have been privileged to see through all the ages, and the despair, the empty feeling of helplessness that had weighed me down, curiously was lessened.

I returned to a scrutiny of the tower. I counted the Plebos under Daster's command on the high platform. Twenty-six. It was more difficult to count those below, but I saw there were certainly in the near neighborhood of fifty. Ten were with Gohret, guarding the Matra and one was dead. Originally, I recalled, there had been a hundred.

That left only a handful unaccounted for, not more than fifteen certainly. Where were these?

Blurred movement at the edge of the disk seemed to offer an answer. I shifted it to bring the movement near its center —

"Good Lord!" I exclaimed. "Look at that."

The movement I'd glimpsed was at the entrance aperture to the House of Earth. There were coming out of it no Plebos, but the giant Norseman, light glinting from his winged metal casque, and the blonde Briton. Streaming after them came the Roman in his toga, the vividly garmented Egyptian, the Mongol Lieutenant of Genghis Khan, all the humans who'd congregated in the room from which Daster had called me and my companions.

They started running, toward the Future Men at the base of the tower! Something flashed through the air ahead of them and a Plebo on the fringe of the cluster nearest them toppled, an arrow quivering in the back of his enormous head. The Redskin who'd dispatched that arrow fitted another to his bow. The bare, muscular arm of a patrician-featured Greek swept back to launch a javelin.

"They're attacking!" Evelyn cried. "They're charging the Future Men!"

"If they capture and destroy the tower . . ."

The Viking came on in great bounds, swinging a two-handed sword broader even than Excalibur. The Roman's, close beside him, was a short blade little longer than a knife. The Greek's javelin arced over their heads, found its mark in another Plebo's eye —

Passed right through and left the Plebo, standing, unaffected!

"Damn!" I grunted. "Now that the Future Men know they're

coming those things can do no more harm to them than Orth's bullet to Daster."

The Indian's second arrow swept harmlessly through the defenders of the tower. A stone axe hurled by a pelt-clothed Pict might have been thrown at shadows, for all the effect it had. The Plebos were facing the charge, their weapons in their hands now, weapons like those with which the ones guarding the Matra were armed. The very calmness with which they awaited the attack gave proof of how little they feared it. But the Norseman came on, waving his sword, his walrus mustaches drooped on either side of a mouth wide open to vent a bellow of defiance I could not hear. The attacking column rushed toward the menace of the Plebos' mysterious weapons and not one of the motley assortment that composed it hestitated or turned to flee.

"They are fools," I heard Villon voice what was in my mind. "But what magnificent fools!"

Or were they? The Plebos held their fire and the Viking, still foremost, was within ten yards of them. Did the charging men have a chance? If they had, if they captured the tower — The wing-helmeted head vanished from the Norseman's shoulders! The Roman's sword arm was sheared off clean at the joint and his abruptly legless torso thudded down, quiveringly, horribly still alive. The Egyptian was sliced in half, a slashed fragment of the Indian skidded across the plaza . . .

It was over. There had been no flashes from the Plebos' weapons. There had been no evidence that they'd done any thing but stand there and wait for the charge to reach them, yet there no longer was any charge. Nothing was left of those who'd attacked with such magnificent courage save scarcely recognizable fragments of human bodies scattered over the rocky plain.

There was no blood. It seemed especially horrible that they did not bleed.

"Take them, Oh Eternal," Elijah droned. "Take their bright souls to Thy bosom and give them eternal rest."

"Amen," I whispered, and I heard a whispered amen from Orth and Louis, from Arthur and Evelyn. None of us could possibly have spoken above a whisper, for a long moment.

The throbbing silence was broken by Villon. "And that, my friend," he was not smiling, "is what awaits us in the chamber where the Matra lies."

"Nevertheless, poet," I growled, "I'm going to have a try at making our friends of the future pay for what they've just done out there."

"You were going to find the controls for the Veil," Evelyn's soft voice reminded me.

That brought me back a little to myself. I blotted out the scene outside the House of Sun, drew the probing rays of the television disk within it, started scanning its every nook and cranny.

It was a vast labyrinth of passages, a warren of rooms large and small. Some of the rooms were empty, some piled to the ceiling with all kinds of things that I should like to have examined more closely. I went on and on, grimly searching for the vulnerable heart of Adalon's defences.

I had begun at the lowermost level of the immense structure, and now my search had reached the base of the dome that surmounted it, and as yet I had not found that for which I hunted.

The great stratcar hangar came into the disk. Only one of the silvery fliers remained there; all the rest, I guessed, had gone out to fight the drina and had been wrecked. I tried to recall how many there had been. About a dozen. Each of the missing ones must have been ridden by at least one Plebo. There still were four or five to be located. They must be somewhere.

The disk moved slowly in my hand. It was grayed by the momentary blankness I had learned meant that the beam, or whatever it was that scanned the distant scenes, was passing through a wall. The grayness cleared and I was looking at a vaulted room fully as large as that where the stratcars had been.

This, however, was not like the hangar, hollow and empty. It was packed with a maze of gleaming metal, of glowing tubes and looped cables, the whole vibrating so that I could almost hear the hum of leashed energy.

"This is it," I said hoarsely. "This is their powerhouse."

Here, for the first time anywhere in the House of Sun except the room where the Matra slept, I found life. A single Plebo paced around the intricacy, his enormous eyes intent upon it.

"One," Villon murmured. "There is only one." From the corner of my eye I saw that he fingered the hilt of his poniard. "Wait," I said. "Wait, Villon."

At one end of the plexus of polished steel and copper the cables joined and formed a huge coil, something like the intricate induction coils of a radio except that this was perhaps a hundred yards in diameter. No conductor left it. All the energy that was being created here was being fed into this, and apparently remained there.

That was queer, I thought, then recalled what Daster had told me of the manner in which the Future Men used their own brains as electrical machines. It dawned on me that they mentally tapped this reservoir of power and directed it to where it was needed.

That was that. I could not get at the controls of the Veil of Ishlak because those controls were the minds of the Doctils themselves. Wait! I did not have to worry about the controls! The energy that formed the Veil originated in that room and if we could reach it, if we could destroy the prime power-source it housed, the Veil would collapse.

The Veil would collapse and the drina would pour down into Adalon. They would surge over the Doctils and over the Plebos.

And over us. Over Evelyn.

I recalled what I had seen on the entrance plain. I recalled the linked armor that still held the empty shape of a man. Not even that much would be left of the honey-haired girl, the gray-eyed girl whose lips I had tasted and found sweet.

There was that other room. The room where Gohret and his Plebos watched over the Matra.

I had just seen what folly the thought of a frontal attack on them was. To think of reaching the Matra by stealth was as futile. Her case was in the chamber's very center, the unbroken circle of Plebos around it and Gohret beside it. Only an Adalonian could even enter that room in safety. Now if only I could assume Astaris' shape as easily as he had mine —

Maybe that wasn't necessary. Maybe — "It's worth a try," I said aloud.

"What's worth a try, Johnny?" Evelyn inquired. "What are you thinking about?"

I turned to her, drinking in that slender body of hers, etching on my memory its delicate curves, the translucent oval of her face. I had come to a decision and I had only a few moments more to capture an image of her to take with me into oblivion.

"Johnny." Her hand was in mine. "Why don't you answer me? You've figured out something. Why don't you tell us what it is?"

"Yes, dear. I've figured out a way of getting at the Matra that has a one-in-a-million chance of coming off. But before I talk about that, I want to arrange for the second string to our bow, the lifting of the Veil. I'm sure that can be done."

The others were looking at me now, their eyes questioning.

"Francois," I said. "You were watching the disk as closely as I was. Do you think that you can find the room where the great machine is?"

"Of a surety, my cabbage. That is very simple for one who could travel the roofs of the Faubourg St. Germaine on nights when even the squawling cats were blind, and in all that myriad of windows find the one behind which slept the maiden to whom his current fancy drew him."

"Fine. Because I want you to lead them there, Elijah and Orth and Louis, and Evelyn. Arthur too, carrying Astaris with him. When you get near it, you will leave the others and sneak into that place and use your poniard on the Plebo in there."

A crooked grin crossed the Frenchman's face. "Understood, my carrot."

"When you've disposed of him, call in the others. And wait."

"Wait? For what?"

"You'll know. Because I'm going to give you this television disk to take along — here Louis, you'd better carry it — and in it you will watch the room of the Matra. What you see happen there will tell you, Arthur," I turned to him and Orth, "whether to smash the lights you will see glowing here and there about the machine in that room."

"To smash lights." Arthur's brows gathered in puzzlement. "And why should you set us to smashing lights, John March?"

"If you are discovered," I ignored his question for the moment, "don't stop to fight but smash those lights. Because," now I answered the king, "when they are smashed the power will be shut off from the Veil of Ishlak and there no longer will be a Veil to hold back the drina and so there will be no point in fighting.

"Orth," I continued, trying not to see the effect of that on them, "give me your gun. Francois, after we are out in the corridor I shall want the thing you took from the Plebo you killed, the 'key' as you call it."

"Why, Johnny?" Evelyn broke in, her eyes widening. "What are you going to do?"

"I'm going to try to get to the room of the Matra, darling, and I'm going to try to kill her. The chances are a million to one against my succeeding, but if I do succeed, in time, you will have a chance to live."

"And you?"

"Oh," I shrugged, "I'll make out all right." And quickly, so that she should not read in my eyes that I lied, that whether I killed the Matra or not I would surely die, I turned to the Dauphin. "Louis. It will be your job to act as lookout to warn the others of the approach of any Plebos or Doctils. And, my boy, if and when it becomes necessary for the lights to be smashed, to warn them of the approach of the drina."

Now I was almost finished. I had only one more instruction to give. "Francois. A word in private with you, if the others will not mind."

We stepped aside and I murmured what I had to say in his ear. He heard it, and blinked at me, and then I thought he stood a little more erect, a little more proudly than before. "John," he murmured. "John Marsh. I have received the accolades of counts and dukes, of a king and a Pope but never, in my misspent life have I been honored as thus at its end you honor me."

What I had told him was that if it came to it that Louis warned of the drina's approach, he was gently, very gently, to slip his poniard into Evelyn's heart.

CHAPTER 25

TO DIE ALONE

A SOFT THUD SWUNG ME TO KING Arthur. His sheathed sword was lifting from Astaris' enormous head.

"The varlet stirred," the king explained, "and we had to quiet him."

I stared down at the Doctil, grotesque, malignant even lying there bound and unconscious. If in that instant of dawning awareness, he'd sent out even one syllable of a cry for help, my million to one chance of getting to the Matra and gaining for Evelyn a slim hope of survival was gone.

There was no way of telling whether he had sent out that appeal.

Villon's arm was across my shoulder. "John," his low voice murmured. "Indeed there is peril for all of us, but for the task of greatest peril you have appointed yourself. You are young. You have the love of that sweet maiden to live for. For me, even were I to return to my land and my epoch, there is nothing left but a dreary exile, poverty, the haunted skulking of an outcast. Let me take your place, and you mine."

"Thank you, Francois," I answered. "But it isn't any melodramatic heroism that motivates me. If what I'm going to try to do can be done at all, only I can do it. I'm the only one who possibly can hope to get near the Matra. We're wasting time. Let's get started."

I was sure that the 'key' would take two at a time through the wall, and I didn't want to risk experimenting with more. Our exodus to the corridor, therefore, took longer than I liked, Villon ferrying us through one by one. I went first, to stand on guard with Orth's gun, and each time Francois vanished into the stone, I wondered whether before he returned I should see a squad of Plebos hurrying toward us, through simple bad luck or brought by some call from our prisoner. My palms were wet with cold sweat by the time Arthur appeared with the stunned Doctil across his shoulder so for the sake of doing something I took the 'key' from him myself and went back to bring Francois out.

I dropped it into my vest pocket when we were in the corridor again, and saluted the men. They moved away, rounded the curve of the corridor where it lifted upward to continue its long spiral, passed from sight. I was alone with Evelyn for the last time.

I dared take only a minute for our parting, dared not trust myself to speak. Nor was it with words that she told me that my love for her was no greater than hers for me.

Then Evelyn Rand was going away from me, to join the others who were waiting for her, and I was really alone. Forever. I turned, started down the long, winding incline towards where, as surely as though I myself had drawn the plans of the House of Sun, I knew I would find the cell of the Matra and those who waited with death in their hands for any enemy who might try to approach her.

I wasn't afraid of what lay ahead. One is no longer afraid when one knows that death is imminent and inevitable.

I went over what I contemplated. I would have to rehearse my every act, my every movement so that they would follow one another precisely, mechanically. If I had to think, even for an instant, I would fail. That was —

My hand flashed to Orth's gun in my pocket as I whirled to a footfall behind me — "Eve!" burst from my lips. "My God, Eve. What-?"

She slipped her fingers into the crook of my elbow. "You didn't think I would let you go alone, Johnny," she smiled. "You didn't really think I would let you die, without me at your side to die with you." There was a glint of mischief in her eyes, a mischievous twist at the corners of her mouth. "I waited till I was sure you had gone too far to send me back, and then I came after you."

"You little fool. You dear little fool. You'll ruin every —" I checked. Her being with me wouldn't ruin my plan. It might even help it.

"What are we going to do, Johnny?" she asked. "What's' your plan?"

I had to tell her. I had to be sure that she understood it in every detail. "It's very simple, my dear. I'm going to pretend to be Astaris."

"Astaris! But you can't make yourself look like him."

"I don't have to. He made himself look like me. Gohret knows that, doesn't know he's changed back. He doesn't know that I've got hold of one of the instruments that enable the Plebos to go through the walls. When I come through the wall into that room, he'll be almost certain, in the first instant, to think I'm Astaris."

"In the first instant. But he can read our thoughts, Johnny. He'll read yours, and since you know that you're really John March he'll know it too, at once."

"That's the weakest point of my scheme. But I think can get past it."

"How?"

"*By being* Astaris. By convincing myself that I am Astaris, as a great actor convinces himself that he is the character he portrays; so that every unconscious gesture of his is that character's and not his own. I'm no actor, the Lord knows, but now I have to be one and I will."

"I know you will, Johnny." Her quiet trust in me gave me renewed confidence. "I know you will. But, Astaris, why should you keep your disguise as March when you're going to Gohret?"

"Whoa up, Eve. You don't know that I'm Astaris. You still think I'm John March. You've asked a question that was bothering me till you showed up but now it's answered. Here's the story. I assumed John March's personality, his whole make-up, in the hope that your love would evoke a corresponding emotion in me. You see, I can't conceive that it is anything but a physical or chemical reaction, requiring only a duplication of conditions to come about. Well, I've succeeded. I've learned the nature of love. Under normal conditions I would bring you before the whole Kintat to confirm it, but because the others are occupied with the defense against the drina, I'm taking you to Gohret alone.

"If I changed back to my real form, you would be terrified, and the experiment ruined. I might even lose the effect it has had on me. That's why I'm still posing as John March. Do you understand?"

Her brow wrinkled, adorably. "It's a little complicated. You're Astaris, and you want Gohret to know that, but you want me to think that you're my Johnny."

"Exactly. I'm posing as Astaris posing as me. I am Astaris posing as John March. Your part is easy. You know I'm John March, and you're very much in love with me. You don't understand what I'm up to but you trust me implicitly."

"In other words I just have to be myself."

"Exactly. You can even be as scared as you please of Gohret and the Plebos. You only have to be careful to remember to forget what happened in that garden back there."

"You mean when you —"

"Hold it, darling. I kissed you in the garden, and we were very happy with our love, so that you almost forgot all the strange things that had been happening until then. I asked you to come somewhere with me, and you answered that you would go anywhere as long as it was with me, anywhere in the world or out of it. You're a little startled because you have suddenly found yourself in this corridor. You'll be somewhat more startled when I've taken you into the room of the Matra, and you'll be terrified of Gohret, but you will depend on me to take care of you. Come on, my very dear. We've got only a little farther to go. And trust me."

"Yes, Johnny, dear. I trust you always and forever."

She has no suspicion that I am Astaris, I thought. She trusts me, and she loves me. Queer. This feeling I have towards her, drawing me to her, thrilling me at the very touch of her, is baffling. Something electrical in its nature, something chemical. I can't quite analyze it, using March's brain. If I could use my own — I'd better not, just yet. I don't have to. Gohret will examine us, both of us, and he'll know exactly what change she has made in me. Ah. We're here, outside the Room of the Matra. I hope that her terror over what she'll see in it won't mask her love-reactions from Gohret. Well, that's a chance I have to take. But I'll try to prepare her for what awaits her.

"We're going through this door, dear," I said aloud. "There will be things inside you won't understand, but trust me, no harm is going to come to you."

"I'm not afraid, Johnny," she answered. "As long as I'm with you. But kiss me, before you open that door."

I took her in my arms, the way I'd seen it done so many times, in so many different centuries, and I pressed my lips against hers. Her slender body was trembling in the circle of my arms, and her lips were cold on mine. Mine were cold too, and there was a tightness around my brow. That was because this was the crucial moment of my experiment, and I was really quite worried lest it fail. Strange how this love business makes one susceptible to other emotions too, how it weakens one's philosophical attitude toward all the phenomena of nature.

I took her arms tenderly from about my neck. "We've got to go in, darling," I said. I took her hand in mine. My fingers slid into my vest pocket and, standing close to the wall, I pressed against it. We were going through the wall. We were in the Room of the Matra. The guards circled the crystal case, and Gohret stood above it, thinking how much depended on the white, sleeping form within it.

The Plebos were startled. Their weapons came up. "Gohret!" I sent the thought to my brother Doctil, proud a little of my triumph. "My experiment has succeeded. I want you to examine the change in me, but be careful not to disturb the female."

Aloud, I said, as Evelyn Rand might expect John March to say, "You sent for us, Mister. What do you want?" And I kept moving toward the center of the room.

We were moving straight on the lifted weapons of the Plebos. The fools. They look uncertain. They are about to loose their rays. Is my pose as John March too well done? Don't they, doesn't Gohret, believe that I am Astaris?

John March's hand closed on the butt of the gun in the pocket of his jacket, and his fingers curled over its trigger.

CHAPTER 26

VENGEANCE

EVELYN RAND'S FEET DRAGGED. There was no color in her face and her eyes were dark pits in its pallor. Gohret's thoughts were unformed, puzzled, as he stood motionless above the bed of the Matra and watched us come toward him.

They became clearer. "Something wrong, something blurred, in the way he communicates with me I do not recognize Astaris' mind." "That is because my mind uses the cells of March's brain," I answered him, silently. "I am surprised that you do not comprehend it." I was beginning to be a little angry at his stupidity, at the insolence of the Plebos who stood steadfast, blocking me. Me, a Doctil! They were blocking my way no longer. Two had moved aside to let us pass.

We were on the platform. We were within a long pace of the Matra's case. *John March's gun moved a bit to aim at the form within it-*

Gohret's right tentacle lashed forward! *March's finger squeezed the trigger!* The Doctil grabbed my arm in that exact moment. I saw the case smash into splinters, I saw a red splotch on the Matra's temple. "Goodbye, Eve!" I gasped, as the Plebos whirled to cut us down — Darkness smashed into the room, utter, impenetrable darkness!

Gohret's reaching arm found me, and I pounded it with the butt of the gun, out of my pocket now. "The power!" I sensed his startled thought. "All power's off!" All about me was a jumble of panic, the Plebos' dismay, their confusion. I knew they were trying to ray me down, but nothing was happening. Nothing was happening because their weapons no longer tapped the energy that would have sliced us to pieces as we'd seen the charging men sliced, out on the floor of the Bowl.

Keeping tight hold of Evelyn I lurched toward where I recalled the wall was, was using Orth's gun as a club to batter the unseen Plebos out of my way. Confused, panicky, they were blundering into one another, into us. Gohret's mind was searching for us, but we were screened from it by the terror of the Plebos, by their silent shouts, "The Veil. The Veil of Ishlak is gone. The drina are coming." Abruptly I was through their heaving mass, was staggering across a free space, Eve still in the circle of my arm.

"It wasn't any use," I gasped. "We've killed the Matra, but Arthur had smashed the machines." We thudded into something hard, vertical. "We've saved our world, but we're through. The drina will get us."

"We've saved our world, Johnny," I heard her answer. "And we can die happy. Like this." Her lips trailed across my cheek, found mine and clung to them.

"No." I pulled my head back from hers. "Maybe the books are closing on us, but we aren't dead yet." I was fishing in my vest-pocket. "We're not giving up. If we're going to die, we'll die trying." I didn't have any hope the 'key' would get us through the wall now, with no energy-flux for it to tap, but I was going to try it. "The drina haven't gotten us yet."

There were two small objects in my pocket. One of them was the key. The other — I brought them both out — the other, I recalled, was the black gem that I'd found in Evelyn Rand's room in Westchester and had carried ever since.

"Put your arm around my waist, Eve," I directed. I held the gem in my left hand while I put the key against the vertical rock and squeezed it.

Nothing happened. Well, I had expected that. We were done for. We'd stay here till the drina found us —

We wouldn't be alive when the drina found us. Gohret was coming toward us! In the same curious manner that I'd been able to hear their unspoken words, I knew that he'd succeeded in quieting the Plebos, had located us, and was coming to take revenge on us for the death of the Matra. He was no longer the cold, intellectual man of the future. He was white hot with rage, with fury, and he wasn't going to leave us for the drina. I turned to meet him —

Started to turn! The floor heaved — threw me against the wall. I shoved both hands against it, to save myself from falling. The black stone in my left hand clicked on the rock, and there was a sharp, tearing sound. Dim, brownish light jagged the blackness of the wall and there was dust in my nostrils. The break in the facade widened, and I half fell through it.

Evelyn fell with me into the spiral corridor. Its floor heaved as I spun to meet the menace of the Doctil — was just in time to see the cleft in the wall through which we'd come closed by rock fragments tumbling into it, to see them crush in Gohret's ungainly skull. Evelyn's little fists were pounding my back. "The drina, Johnny," she screamed above a shrill vibration of sound that till now I had been unaware of. "Look."

The brownish light came in through the aperture at the end of the long ramp out of which Daster, long ago, had led me from the House of Sun. That aperture was jagged-edged now, was growing wider as I glimpsed it. Was being made wider by amorphous, purple-gray tendrils tearing at its rocky frame, tearing the stone from it in great chunks. A purple-gray sea surged out there beyond it, and it was from this sea that the shrill, ear-piercing whistle rose.

"Good Lord!" I grunted. "The projectors on the tower were useless when the power was cut off, and there was nothing at all to hold back the drina. They've swallowed all the Future Men out there, and now they're tearing this building apart to get at the few left inside here — and us. That's why it's shaking so, as if it were in the grip of an earthquake. It's curtains for us —"

"Not yet, Johnny. Their tearing at the building was what broke the cleft in the wall, and saved us from Gohret. Don't you get some hope from that?"

"I don't see —"

"Johnny!" Evelyn shook me. "You said we'd die trying."

"Yeah," I grunted. "But what's there left to try? Look. They're coming" The aperture large enough, a purple-gray mass was oozing through it. "And they're tearing the whole building down over our heads. Wait! They can't tear the whole building down all at once, it's too huge. It will take them a long time. There's one thing we can still try. If we can get to the top ahead of them, if that stratcar can still fly — Come on!"

We were running up that steep, winding incline. We were running endlessly. Behind us, and below, was the shrill and terrible whistle of the drina, and the thud of falling stone, and abruptly there was a great scream in my mind, a soundless scream that I knew to be the death cry of the Plebos whom we'd left behind in the Room of the Matra.

And then the scream was ended, and there was only the shrill whistle of the drina, and that was fading, and the shuddering of the floor under our feet had diminished to an almost imperceptible vibration. We were running, endlessly running in the sightless dark, endlessly circling, endlessly climbing.

My legs ached, every muscle, every sinew a separate, tearing pain. An iron band about my chest constricted my lungs and each gasping breath sliced them. My temples pounded —

Evelyn wasn't beside me any longer.

I halted, turned back. "Eve!" I gasped. "Eve!"

No answer. No sight of her in that absolute darkness.

I started back, groping. "Eve!" I mustn't pass her in the dark. "Eve!" I staggered from side to side of the passage to make sure I would not pass her. "Eve, darling." My feet thudded against something soft, and I went to my knees.

"Johnny." It was barely audible. "I can't . . . run any longer. Kiss me . . . Johnny . . . and go."

I bent forward and kissed her. And then I was working my arms under her, to lift her. I couldn't. I no longer had the strength. I couldn't lift Eve. I couldn't carry her to safety.

Well, this was as good a place as any to die. I settled down, like that, her warm body in my arms, the softness of her against my chest, my lips on hers in a long, long kiss.

Very faintly I began to hear the drina's shrill whistle. They were coming. They were coming up the black spiral. Very slowly they were coming, and they had a long way to come, but they'd get here.

I was tired. So tired . . .

CHAPTER 27

DUST UNTO DUST

SOMETHING SEIZED ME, TORE ME from Eve, lifted me. I cried out some unintelligible gibberish, batted feebly at that which had taken hold of me —

"'Tis he, by my halidom," a familiar voice boomed. "'Tis our John March." King Arthur's great voice. John Orth's guttural tones, answering him. "And the Fraulein Evelyn."

"Arthur," I managed to whisper. "What? How . . . ?"

"We essay to sortie from this castle, the Archduke and I," he answered "The others preferred to await their fate above."

"You can't get out, Arthur. You'll have to go back. Listen. Do you hear that whistling sound?" It was only a little louder. "The drina are making that. They're coming up the passage. You can't get past them."

"Back it is, then." He started off, carrying me. "Follow, Duke Orth."

"Let me down," I said feebly. "I can walk."

"Nay. Layest thou quietly in our arms, John. Thou art but hardly able to make thyself heard. Thou hast not strength to make this exceeding great climb but we have the strength for both. Lie still, and let thy king carry thee."

There wasn't any use in arguing with him. "What happened, Arthur? Why did you smash the machinery? Didn't you see in the disk that we'd gotten into the room of the Matra? Why didn't you give us a few seconds more?"

"Nay an that we would have, had we been able. The Frenchman had slain the single guard, and we were gathered in the chamber where the magical contrivances buzzed like an hundred hives of bees, all but the lad Louis who guarded without as thou hadst commanded him. We watched thee in that Satan's circle, marvelling that the demons permitted thee to pass through their ranks, that the orange-clad ogre seemed to greet thee amicably but in that instant the lad cried out, 'Plebos! Ware Plebos!' and instanter I with *Excalibur,* the duke and the Jew and the Frenchman with their bare hands, shattered the witch lights that shone there.

"In the sudden night we leaped upon the demons already within the chamber. Then, indeed, Excalibur proved its worth. The unequal combat was over and done with in a trice. No quarter was asked in that fray, and none given."

"How about Astaris?"

"He remaineth our prisoner."

I would have asked more, but just then the passage curved and levelled out, and ahead a wavering yellow light silhouetted Elijah's tall, bearded form and cast a wavering glimmer on the faces of Villon and the Dauphin, who seemed absorbed in something the poet was telling him. The light came from a small, extremely smoky fire on the floor. "We each gave some article of our apparel," Arthur explained it. "And Duke Orth set flame to them with fire dust he beareth with him."

"Powder for that gun of mine," the Austrian made clear.

"Let me down," I told Arthur. "I'm all right now." This time he took my word for it and so I was on my own feet when Villon spied me.

"John!" He bounded toward me, and before I could prevent him, had kissed me on the cheeks. "John! Mourning you for dead, I was about to compose an elegy for you. And Evelyn," he turned to her. "The white flower of all man's dreams! Now indeed, Elijah my bearded rabbi, I begin to have some credence in the efficacy of your heathen prayers."

"We still need those prayers, Elijah. Listen." I lifted my hand. The whistle of the drina came clearly from the passage that had led us here. "We've got just about five minutes to find some way out of here, and I don't know what that could be, unless the stratcar's still working. Is there any way we can get into the hangar?"

"We've searched. Its walls are solid — But you have the 'key', John!"

"I have it." Somehow I'd held on to it all this time. "But it isn't any good." I held it out to him. "Want it for a souvenir —" It was my left hand I had held out. The black thing on its palm was not the 'key,' but the carved gem.

"How came you by this?" It was Elijah who demanded that, staring down at the thing. There was something of surprise, something almost of awe, in his face. "How came you by it?"

"Why?" I asked. "What is it?"

"The very basis of the Kabbala," the prophet answered me. "The very essence of all its philosophy. Look you." He pointed at it. "The Snake of Life, swallowing its own tail, and therefore without beginning and without end. His coils wind in and out in symbol that the spirit of the Godhead, no matter how twisted, no matter through how many planes of existence, how many layers of time and space it passes, returns always upon itself, and is always of one nature, one being. Israel possessed this before my time, and before my time it was lost! How come you by it, John March?"

"I found it in Eve's room."

Elijah turned to her, but it was to me she said, "You gave it to me, Johnny."

"What!"

She smiled wanly. "I mean the play-friend I called Johnny gave it to me. At least, I found it on my dresser one day, after he'd gone. I don't know where it could have come from."

"It was I who left it there." No voice this but a brain-echo I knew must come from a Doctil. From Astaris, the only Doctil still alive. "I found it on this planet, Evelyn Rand, and I left it with you when you were a child so that I should know you again when you had grown old enough to be brought here." He stood beside me, his broken bonds at his feet. "When I had brought you here I replaced it where I had first left it to mark for me the man you were destined to love."

The nape of my neck prickled. Astaris had brought the gem to Earth from this planet, yet Elijah had recognized it as a sacred symbol of the creed that was among the very first on Earth to proclaim the Oneness of God. It was made of the selfsame substance as the awesome monument of the Being the drina worshipped, yet a million years before there had been any contact between Earthman and drina, it, or something so like it that the Prophet in Israel had been able at once and fluently to interpret its intricate message, had existed on Earth. There was meaning beneath meaning in the carved gem. Was it, I asked myself, by accident that the wall of the Matra's room had split for Evelyn and me precisely where I had struck it with the gem—?

"The drina!" The Dauphin's cry broke in upon these thoughts. *"Messieurs,* the drina are upon us," and the shrill whistle of the drina pierced my ears and their slither was very loud against the spiral tunnel's walls.

I twisted to where it debauched into the room, saw the first gray-purple psuedopod squirm in, saw Arthur leap to it, saw *Excalibur* flash above his blonde locks and slash down.

The jelled and terrible mass quivered in the doorway, hesitant. "Take the maid, my old," Villon whispered to me, his smile still holding the twisted and bitter mockery with which it greeted life and death alike. "Retreat with her behind the great engine and do there what you must. We will defend you as long as we may." Then he was beside the king, his poniard hacking at a renewed surge of the drina as Orth thrust a twist of powder, a bullet into my hand, whirled and with a bar snatched from somewhere had joined the others.

As I feverishly reloaded Orth's pistol, I saw Elijah flailing the dark protoplasmic surge with a black length of wrist-thick cable. The gun was ready and I looked for Evelyn, found her wrestling with the Dauphin who struggled to break her hold and join the hopeless battle against the *drina*. I saw her eyes widen with horror abruptly, saw the boy break loose and dive headlong to where a slow wave rolled over the Archduke and engulfed him.

Arthur already was gone, but the white-maned patriarch and the poet still fought, giving back step by reluctant step from the horror — it was utterly useless to fight but that somehow they slowed in its inexorable advance. "Evelyn," I called. "Eve," and as she came about to me strong in my nostrils was the perfume that had been all I'd known of her for so long, the fragrance of a terrestrial spring that neither of us would ever know again. "Eve, darling," I said. "There is only one more thing I can do for you." Raising the pistol, taking careful aim, I said. "You understand, I know."

I read comprehension in her gray eyes and thanks and love. I heard Elijah drone the prayer a devout Hebrew prays when he is about to die, and I heard the prayer silenced. I heard Villon cry, "Farewell, John and Evelyn. Fare you very —" and that cry was blotted out. I gritted my teeth for the pull on the trigger that would give Evelyn a clean death —

"No!" Astaris' voice in my brain forbade the shot. "No, John March. Wait!"

I'd forgotten him, but now in that blazing instant our minds were one and I knew that he had the power to save himself or us but not himself *and* us.

"I am sending you back, John Marsh. You — and Evelyn Rand."

His experiment had been successful. He had set out to learn love and he had. He'd learned love and in learning love he'd learned sacrifice.

A scream of ultimate anguish threaded blue-edged through my brain — but it was not from Evelyn it came, nor from me. We were wrapped in sudden darkness. Not darkness. An absence of color, of form, of reality itself. We were falling through nothingness. We were caught up in some unimaginable maelstrom, we were whirling down and down in a spaceless, timeless nonexistence.

All about us was the soft and voiceless whisper of whirling dust.

CHAPTER 28

THE FORK IN TIME'S RIVER

A WHORL OF DUST SWIRLED AWAY from us down the country road and faded into the gray and quiet light of dusk.

Cicadas began their shrill piping in the thickets. The evening star twinkled in the sky's darkening blue and I turned to Evelyn. "We're home, Eve," I murmured. "We're home again, dear heart. In our own time. In our own world."

"Home, Johnny." She opened the gate and a faded, tenuous voice came to us out of the dusk. "Come, Evelyn. Come in and bring your young man with you. Come in to Faith who's been waiting a long time for you."

The voice came from the porch of a great house that glimmered whitely in the dusk. Faith Corbett, so shrunken and fragile that it seemed a not too high wind must blow her away was calling from the open door that framed a rectangle of light, warm and welcoming. Hand in hand Evelyn and I went up the path to the house where a lonely child with curls the hue of honey used to play with the Johnny of her dreams.

It seemed natural that supper waited piping hot for us on the table in a high-ceiled dining room walled with dark and lustrous oak. It seemed so natural that it was not till we sat side by side on the cushioned sofa before the great fireplace in the parlor that Evelyn thought to ask Faith Corbett how she'd known to have the house ready for us, how she'd known we were coming home.

"I knew," she smiled faintly. "When John talked with me in my cottage I knew then that he would find you and that he would bring you home in two days."

"Two days, Faith!" I exclaimed. In that Otherwhere it had seemed but a few hours. "Are you sure it is two days since I talked with you?"

"Aye, I am sure," her thin voice answered. "That was Sunday afternoon and this is Tuesday night." And then she was rustling out of that drowsy room, so bent and shrunken and old that she seemed a wraith from some, Otherwhere herself, and left us to the red leap of the fire and to the peace of our being together with no fear brooding in our hearts and no doom overhanging us and our world.

Eve stirred in my arms, after a while. "Johnny," she murmured. "It — it was all a dream, wasn't it. I dreamed it."

"No, dear heart. You didn't dream it. It was very real. It —" my brow puckered. "I — I'm not so sure. It's getting so vague now. It does seem as though I dreamed it. But we couldn't both have had the same dream. That isn't possible."

"How do we know it was the same dream, Johnny?" Eve asked. The scent of her was in my nostrils, the redolence of spring and the evasive fragrance of dreams. "Suppose we tell each other what we remember, and then we'll know whether it was the same — the same nightmare we both had."

"No, darling. We won't talk about it any more. Not tonight. But I'll write it all out, and you'll read what I've written and tell me whether it checks with your memories."

And so, when at last we went up to the rooms Faith Corbett had prepared for us, airing them, warming the sheets, I did not go to sleep but sat down at an old desk to write what I could remember. This that you have read is what I wrote that night, and all the next day, and all the next night, and when I read it over after I'd finished, it was all quite as new to me as it was to you.

And Evelyn had no memory at all of any of her part in the narrative.

Now this might seem to prove that it was only a particularly vivid nightmare that I had had, except for this. Evelyn cannot tell me where she was between Sunday, January 26th and Tuesday, February 11th of this year nor has the most diligent search unearthed for us anyone who saw her between when the doorman of her apartment house watched her set out for church and when Faith called to us from the doorway of her old home in Westchester. And none of my friends, my acquaintances can be found who saw hide or hair of me on Monday the 10th or Tuesday, the 11th.

I have been able to locate the entrance guard of a certain art gallery on Madison Avenue, the owner of a second hand bookstore on the same thoroughfare, a policeman who was on post near that bookstore Monday before noon and a taxi driver. All four of these men recall me and the latter three recall exactly the details I have set down in this narrative.

Understandably, I think, I did not care to interview the owner of the drugstore on Plum Street.

In addition, I have looked up whatever is known about the other five of us who were taken out of time — if my story is true. There is no question as to the inexplicable disappearances of Francois Villon and John Orth. The incident of Elijah and the pillar of fire is in the Old Testament, of Arthur's passing in the *Morte d'Arthur* and in Tennyson's immortal poem. The evidence as to the Dauphin is confusing. He did vanish from the Paris prison where he had been jailed from the age of nine, but some legends still extant insist that he escaped and lived to a secluded old age on Long Island. But then it will be recalled that I did not actually see Louis die. It is possible that Astaris sent him back to his own time as he did Evelyn and me to ours.

All these circumstances seem to confirm what I have written. There is another concerning which I cannot make up my mind as to whether it verifies or casts doubt on my tale.

One day, not very long ago, Evelyn and I decided to make a pilgrimage to Furman Street, and examine the curious old house at four-nineteen. We took a taxi, and I dismissed it exactly where that other had had its flat.

Now that, to my certain knowledge, was the only previous time I'd ever been in this section of Brooklyn, yet I threaded the maze of those quiet streets with the curious Games of Orange, Pineapple, Cranberry, in absolute certitude, and found Plum without any trouble.

We walked past the drugstore where I seem to have had a weird experience with a card that no one could see but I and started climbing the slope at whose end was the brightness of a blue sky over the water of the bay.

The glorious massing of towers at the end of Manhattan Island rose slowly above the summit of that ascent. "The house is right at the end of this vista," I told Eve. "We'll see it in a moment."

We came to the end of the sidewalk, at Furman Street. Along that waterfront thoroughfare ran the rows of four-storied graystone houses I recalled, exactly as I recalled them. The one to our left had the number, 415, painted on the third step of its high stoop. The one to our right was number 423.

Between them was an iron fence edging a green lawn. The emerald velvet ran to the edge of the retaining wall that keeps Furman Street from tumbling into the East River, and there was no house upon it. None at all.

There was no Four Nineteen Furman Street. There never had been.

I hope this means that the adventure I have related was some strange illusion, that Eve's disappearance for two weeks, mine for two days, has some other explanation. For otherwise there is this disquieting thought to haunt me.

The Kintat of Doctils who will conquer the planet of the drina a million years from now, will believe themselves, their Plebos and their Matra, to be the sole remnant of Mankind. But suppose they are not. Suppose that from among the people of some other Earth City other Doctils, another Matra, will survive the catastrophe. Suppose that these will plan just such a return to the Earth of what to them is the dim past — as Astaris and his fellows will. Suppose that right now they are somewhere among us, spying on us.

Suppose that man in the subway this morning, that man with the strangely yellow skin and the weird, veiled eyes —

"But, Johnny," Evelyn interrupts. She has been reading over my shoulder, a cute trick now, but I'm afraid I shall have to ask her to stop that sort of thing when our honeymoon is over. "If it all really happened, we know the course of history for a million years and we know that no race of Future Men will come back to conquer us in this century or any other."

"We know nothing of the sort," I answer her. "We know nothing about the nature of Time as yet. It might well be that Time is like a great river with many forks down any or all of which the great tide of history may flow. Are we certain that Mankind has only one destiny, the one we saw in the Hall of Midnights Can we be wholly sure that the end of Man inevitably must be that which we saw?"

She has a way, I have learned, of withdrawing into herself when she is thinking, of seeming to be far and far away. She does that now, and now she is back to me, her gray eyes wide. "Johnny. If that's so, Johnny —"

She checks herself. "If it's so," I ask, "what then?"

With her whimsical irrelevance that is not irrelevance at all, she responds, "Remember, Johnny, why the Doctils picked our century for the return to earth? Remember that this was the critical time when what you just called the great tide of history was at a fork in the river of Man's destiny?"

"Yes," I say softly, suspecting what is in her mind but wanting her to put it into words. "Yes, I remember. Go on."

"I can't," Evelyn murmurs, her gray eyes deep and dark with her thoughts. "I can't go on by myself and you and I can't, Johnny, not just the two of us. But maybe all the people of all the world, together, can."

"Can what, Eve?"

"Direct our destiny down the other branch of the fork in Time's river, the branch that will bring our children's children to some brighter and happier future than the dreadful one we saw in that Hall of Midnight."

Her breath catches in her throat and her lip quivers, and she is a child again, a frightened child in the dark. "Can't we, Johnny? Please, Johnny, please say that we can. Please say that we will."

I want to. Very terribly I want to reassure her, but I cannot. I alone, John March alone, cannot tell her which way Man will direct his destiny. It does not rest with me alone to decide.

It is for all of us to make that decision, no matter in what part of the world we dwell, no matter with what tongue we speak, no matter in what manner we worship Him Who looks down upon Earth and upon some planet beyond the furthest galaxy. We still have, or still can recover, Obligation and Loyalty and Faith, and, yes, and Beauty and Love and with these still can direct our destiny to some better goal than the Doctils showed me and Evelyn in that Otherwhere. We still can decide.

But we must make the decision soon. As Pierpont Alton Sturdevant might say, in his lawyer's phrase, Time is of the essence.

THE END

www.ingramcontent.com/pod-product-compliance
Lightning Source LLC
Chambersburg PA
CBHW020131180626
46810CB00004B/1502